Sherlock Holmes
and the
Case of the Fateful Arrow

[Being another manuscript found
in the dispatch box of Dr. John H. Watson,
in the vault of Cox and Co., Charing Cross,
London]

As Edited By

Daniel D. Victor, Ph.D.

(Book Eight in the Series,
"Sherlock Holmes and the American Literati")

Hardcover 978-1-80424-039-7
Paperback ISBN 978-1-80424-040-3
ePub ISBN 978-1-80424-041-0
PDF ISBN 978-1-80424-042-7

Published by MX Publishing
335 Princess Park Manor, Royal Drive,
London, N11 3GX
www.mxpublishing.co.uk

Cover design Brian Belanger

Also by Daniel D. Victor

The Seventh Bullet:
The Further Adventures of Sherlock Holmes

A Study in Synchronicity

Sherlock Holmes and the Shadows of
St Petersburg

The Literary Adventures of Sherlock Holmes,
Volumes 1 and 2

Other Books in the Series,
"Sherlock Holmes and the American Literati":

The Final Page of Baker Street

Sherlock Holmes and the
Baron of Brede Place

Seventeen Minutes to Baker Street

The Outrage at the Diogenes Club

Sherlock Holmes and the London Particular

The Astounding Murder at Cloverwood House

Sherlock Holmes and the Pandemic of Death

For Peter H. Weiner, my dear friend of many years and ever-dependable literary supporter. Were it not for his introducing to me the works of Anna Katharine Green, this book would not only never have been written, but would also not even have existed as a gleam in the eye of its author.

Acknowledgements

Many thanks for their help and continued support to
Judy Grabiner, Peter Weiner, Mark Holzband,
Tom Turley, and Sandy Cohen. And as always, for
her patience and love, additional thanks to my wife,
Norma Silverman.

A note on the text: In addition to the title of the
book, all chapter titles, headnotes, and footnotes
were supplied by the editor.

The Arrow and the Song

I shot an arrow into the air,
It fell to earth, I knew not where;
For, so swiftly it flew, the sight
Could not follow it in its flight.

I breathed a song into the air,
It fell to earth, I knew not where;
For who has sight so keen and strong,
That it can follow the flight of song?

Long, long afterward, in an oak
I found the arrow, still unbroke;
And the song, from beginning to end,
I found again in the heart of a friend.

--Henry Wadsworth Longfellow

American Mystery Writer
Anna Katharine Green (1846-1935)

Prologue

A Letter to Sherlock Holmes

*W*oeful as they were, I had no intention
of ever recounting the particulars of the tragedy. But
once the singular letter arrived, I knew that I would
have to set the record straight. The letter was dated
12 November 1917, a period of great chaos and
darkness in the world. The deadly guns of the Great
War continued to thunder, the horrific casualties at
Passchendaele still tormented, the Spanish Flu began
its insidious crawl into the lungs of the unsuspecting.

Too old to work at the front lines, I did my
part by aiding the wounded who found their way to
us Old Boys at Bart's. Yet in spite of the terrifying
conditions in the fall of '17, the curious epistle
caused me to smile. How ironic that I begin the
account of this unhappiest of Holmes's adventures in
so sanguine a fashion.

The letter in question was handed to me by
my literary agent, Sir Arthur Conan Doyle, between
tankards of ale at the Northumberland Arms, his
favourite public house.* Sir Arthur's appearance in
London that autumn was two-fold. Not only was he
there to deliver one of his lectures about the current

---

* The letter was published in the *Los Angeles Times*, December
16, 1917, p. BR3.

military conflict, but also to engage with his publisher, Hodder and Stoughton, Ltd., concerning the latest volume of his account of the war, *The British Campaign in France and Flanders*. It was in the midst of his negotiations for the third instalment of the history that from seemingly out of the blue he received the letter posted by the American publisher, Dodd, Mead, and Company.

Not that the correspondence was intended for him. "In actuality, Watson," he said in his thick Scottish brogue as he slid the wrinkled envelope across the wooden table, "the letter is for Holmes."

I could read the name on the envelope myself, of course. "To Mr. Sherlock Holmes," the oft-handled cover stipulated in precise penmanship, "care of Sir Arthur Conan Doyle." Turning the envelope over, I observed that its flap, though closed, was unsealed.

"The military censors," Sir Arthur explained. "Since it was already open," he went on to say with a self-conscious pat of his robust moustache, "I confess to having read it myself. Given its nature, Watson, I thought you too might have a look-see before passing it along. I am certain Holmes won't mind, and I am equally certain you'll find it most interesting indeed." This last sentence he uttered with a poorly suppressed chortle.

Accepting the invitation, I placed my tankard on the table and withdrew the epistle from the envelope. To determine its authorship, I immediately glanced at the bottom of the neatly-handwritten page. There I saw the signature of one Ebenezer Gryce, a name not only well-known to

Holmes and me, but especially to readers on the other side of the Atlantic. For many years, Gryce had served as a celebrated detective for the New York Metropolitan Police Force.

It was easy to recognise why Sir Arthur called my attention to the matter. Gryce had begun the letter with an implicit reference to my most recent collection of Holmes's adventures, *His Last Bow*, in whose preface I commented upon my friend's health:

> *My Dear Sherlock Holmes* [Gryce wrote],
> *it is with regret that I learn from a recent notice that you have become afflicted with rheumatism. I trust, however, that it may not seriously interfere with the continuance of your illustrious career.*

By then an octogenarian, Gryce went on to explain that he too suffered from the affliction—a "lame knee" in particular, he had reported elsewhere. It was a malady, he confessed, that had served to hinder many of his investigations, including his most noteworthy, "The Leavenworth Case". Indeed, only with the help of assistants like Mr. Caleb Sweetwater and Mrs. Amelia Butterworth, aides he termed "clever" and "astute," had he been able to solve so many of his most challenging cases.

Proffering "sympathy" and "keen appreciation", the American detective hoped that the rheumatism would not necessitate a "last bow" for Sherlock Holmes. Given Gryce's familiarity with my own contributions to Holmes's work, however, one must assume that his tongue was planted firmly in cheek when he dared recommend how Holmes could cope with his own bouts of rheumatism. To aid in his sleuthing, Gryce recommended that Holmes might, as Gryce had done, secure "some clever fellow as an assistant," a notable figure (not unlike Sir Arthur himself, one suspects).

I should like to believe that many of my faithful readers would take issue with a cheeky New York policeman who calls for an anonymous substitute to fill my role. With due respect to the ongoing war and the emerging Spanish Flu, rather than smiling at such a letter, should I not have joined my defenders in being incensed by so obvious a personal slight?

Yet even the most loyal of my supporters will find me cautioning them to stand down, to breathe deeply, for herein is the rub: As Holmes and I both knew at the time, New York Detective Ebenezer Gryce is a mere fiction, a literary persona concocted by the best-selling American crime writer—a woman, no less—called Anna Katharine Green.

In point of fact, it was the confluence of the differing realities presented in Gryce's letter that elicited my smile. Although one would have had to bury his head in the sand to be unaware of Holmes's numerous victories in fighting crime, such is the nature of his celebrated success that a staggering number of ill-informed readers continue to question the very reality of Sherlock Holmes. Indeed, given the large number of Holmes's triumphs, many such Doubting Thomases have gone so far as to conclude that a hero like Sherlock Holmes could exist only as the figment of someone's imagination.

Why, no less a crime writer than Maurice Leblanc, the originator of the fictional French sleuth, Arsène Lupin, suggested in his story, "The Blonde Woman", that so accomplished a detective as Holmes must doubtlessly be a kind of "legendary figure, a hero who has emerged alive from the mind of a great novelist such as Conan Doyle, for example." With the fictional Ebenezer Gryce making suggestions to the very real Sherlock Holmes, is it any wonder that I was amused?

At the same time, Gryce's letter raises a more serious issue that must also be addressed. The New York detective identified the investigation he titled "The Hasty Arrow" as "an extremely involved matter... [that] gave me no end of concern before it was . . . settled to the satisfaction of the authorities and Miss Green."

One expects nothing less than satisfaction on the part of Miss Green, of course, since it was her own novel, *The Mystery of The Hasty Arrow,* that dramatized the story in the first place. Who else but a book's author can be responsible for its satisfactory conclusion?

What has not been revealed until now, however, is just how much of the romanticised *Hasty Arrow* was based on actual happenings, real events in which Anna Katharine Green had participated whilst helping Sherlock Holmes and me complete a most distressing investigation.

Now I have not made a study of Miss Green's literary techniques, but one cannot deny the charming lady's reputation as an expert in her field. Why, *The Leavenworth Case* alone has sold more than 750,000 copies! Yet it is this very success that made me fearful of revisiting through the lens of a professional novelist the heart-breaking moments upon which her book is based.

Nor was I mistaken. To gain commercial success, Miss Green did indeed embellish, twist, and ultimately distort the haunting details of the original case. In point of fact, it was the distress I experienced in reading the melodramatic *Mystery of the Hasty Arrow* that caused me to take up my own pen in defence of what had actually occurred all those years ago. In deference to the historical record, let this, my own account, serve as an objective report of the painful events that took place in the summer of 1890. The real-life participants earned the right to that respect.

But I anticipate myself. Better to start at the beginning.

John H. Watson, M.D.
London
October 1921

Part I

The British Museum

2 June 1890—3 June 1890

Chapter One

"I Shot an Arrow . . ."

People Love Mystery.
    -- Anna Katharine Green
      "Why Human Beings are
      Interested in Crime"
      American Magazine
      February 1919

"*I*—I saw a young woman shot dead right in front of me," stammered the wide-eyed lady standing at our door. With a gloved hand, she pointed to her chest. "Heart—pierced by an arrow," she gasped, "not three hours ago."

It was early Monday evening, the second day of June, 1890. One does not soon forget the date of so dramatic an encounter.

Mrs. Hudson, who had brought the unnerved woman up the stairs, was shaking her head in sympathy. "This is Dr. Watson," our landlady told her. "He can help you if you're ailing."

"Oh, Dr. Watson," the woman surprised me by taking both of my hands, "you're one of the gentlemen I've come to see."

"I'm afraid—" I began.

"It is I, Doctor," the woman said, pointing to herself once more, "Mrs. Charles Rohlfs. We had agreed to meet one another earlier today."

I am afraid my expression still remained blank.

"The author from New York," she explained, "Ah, you probably know me by my *nom de plume*—Anna Katharine Green."

Of course, I now realised, the celebrated crime writer—her American accent should have informed me. Sherlock Holmes and I had been expecting a visit from this very person many hours earlier—so many hours earlier, in fact, that we had long since given up counting upon her arrival.

"Do come in, Mrs. Rohlfs," said Holmes, who by this time had donned his coat and come to the door. "Pray, tell us what has caused you such consternation."

Mrs. Hudson clucked softly to herself as Mrs. Rohlfs entered; and our landlady, muttering words I could not hear, marched back down the stairs.

Our scheduled meeting had, in fact, been engineered by my agent, Conan Doyle (not yet Sir Arthur). As one who appreciated her detective stories, he had been in written communication with the lady before her current trip to these islands.* Upon learning that she and her family were planning to visit London, Conan Doyle suggested that a meeting with the world's first consulting detective, not to mention the biographer who recorded the detective's investigations, would present a worthwhile professional experience to the lady.

---

* The fictions of Anna Katharine Green were well-known to Conan Doyle. During his tour of the United States in 1894, he wrote to her from the Aldine Club on Fifth Avenue in New York City to arrange a meeting following his lecture in Buffalo where she lived.

"A brandy and soda, Mrs Rohlfs?" Holmes asked our visitor, who still looked a trifle unsteady on her feet.

She smiled in assent, and Holmes nodded in my direction to prompt me to prepare the drink. I had not been gone long enough from Baker Street to have forgotten the benefits of the gasogene. It was by now a practiced habit that when my beloved wife Mary was away from our home for an extended period, I would take the opportunity to reclaim my former room in the flat now occupied only by Holmes. Indeed, on this occasion I had gone so far as to place my medical practice in the hands of a *loco tenens* for the first two weeks of June.

Charming as such a reunion between Holmes and myself might sound, however, bittersweet is the way I experienced it. To be sure, I relished the time shared with my old friend. Yet I also worried about my dear Mary. At that moment she was spending a month with an aunt in the glades of the New Forest to cope with the heart ailment that would ultimately claim Mary's life.

The previous February, my account of Holmes's case, *The Sign of Four,* had been published in *Lippincott's Monthly Magazine.* Readers may recall that in it I described my meeting with the intriguing Mary Morstan, whom I would eventually marry. Only because I was unable to predict her sad fate at the time could I confess without guilt to greatly enjoying my respite with Holmes, including the refreshment he always had at hand.

Once Mrs. Rohlfs and Holmes were seated, I proffered to each a glass of brandy and sparkling water.

"It goes without saying, gentlemen," Mrs. Rohlfs announced after I had settled in with a drink of my own, "that I expected to meet you under different circumstances. But just this afternoon"— here she paused to remove the gloves that covered her arms halfway to the elbow— "I witnessed an innocent young woman struck down by an arrow. *I*," she said, sampling the brandy, "somebody who writes about murders, actually saw one occur just a few hours ago in the British Museum—in an exhibit about the Battle of Hastings. I must confess that the events of the day have overwhelmed me." With a trembling hand, she placed her glass on a side table. "I am still shaken."

"My word," I said, taking some brandy.

"We were expecting a visitor, Watson, but instead we have been delivered a case," said Sherlock Holmes as he steepled his fingers and stretched out his legs. It was a familiar position whenever he sensed the hint of a challenge. "Be so kind, Mrs Rohlfs, as to tell us exactly what happened."

The lady moved her reticule to the side and then appeared to reach above her broad brow for a non-existent hat.

"My goodness," she exclaimed. "In all the excitement I forgot to reclaim my hat. It's on a hook near the museum entrance." With no hat to preoccupy her, she set about adjusting the braided swirl of dark-brown hair that crowned her head.

It was an old-fashioned look in keeping with her sombre, high-collared frock of navy-blue. Though she appeared to be in her forties, her large, blue eyes and round face gave her an almost childlike aspect. Strangely, her writing may have been highly regarded in the current literary world, yet her sense of costume seemed not to have evolved since her youth.

"Well," she said, sampling a bit more of her drink, "we—that is, my family and I—Charles and our two children, Rosamund and Sterling—she's almost five and he's almost three—we arrived in Liverpool two weeks ago. My father died in March of this year, you see, and we thought such a trip to be the very thing to raise our spirits. Can't say that hasn't been the case—until this afternoon, that is." Here she sipped her brandy again. "That poor girl," she muttered, shaking her head.

"We got to London some ten days ago," she went on, "and we've been visiting all the places we Americans hear about—the Tower, your Parliament, Buckingham Palace. I was even extended an invitation to the Society of Authors from Walter Besant, the chairman. Have you ever met him, Doctor?"

"Never had the pleasure," I said. I knew about the prolific novelist and social activist, of course, but attending to my medical practice and recording Holmes's criminal investigations offered scant opportunity to encounter such literary personalities in the flesh.

Talking about her touring experiences seemed to calm Mrs. Rohlfs, yet Holmes exhaled impatiently. "What about today?" he wanted to know. "Pray, provide us with the details that so upset you today."

"Today," she said, raising a forefinger for emphasis, "we left the children in the care of Nelly, their nurse. Charles went off somewhere to examine your English tables and chairs. He enjoys constructing house furnishings, you see—lately, he's been interested in stoves. Right now, it's all just a hobby; but to tell the truth, if his acting career should end, I do think he'd like to spend the rest of his life creating furniture.* If you can believe it," Mrs. Rohlfs added, her pale cheeks turning pink, "a few of his designs include some of the water-colour patterns I've painted for him."

"Yes, yes, Mrs. Rohlfs," said Holmes, "very interesting, I'm sure; but it is this business with the arrow you spoke of that intrigues me—let us hear the facts surrounding it."

"Ah, yes," she said, raising her finger once more. "The plot's the thing—to paraphrase your Bard."

"At last," Holmes muttered. Sitting up and reaching for his black briar, he filled it with shag.

I opened a window in anticipation of the clouds of blue smoke about to arise. For her part, Mrs. Rohlfs leaned forward, smoothed down the folds in her dress, and began her dramatic account.

---

* In the next ten years, Charles Rohlfs would go on to become a world-famous furniture designer as well as a Fellow in the Royal Society of the Arts.

Chapter Two

What Mrs. Rohlfs Saw

Women have more subtle intuitions than men have—
a fact that should make them
valuable in actual detective work.
                    --Anna Katharine Green
                        "Why Human Beings are
                        Interested in Crime"
                        American Magazine, 1919

"*T*here's an exhibition at the British Museum's North Hall that I wanted to see," Mrs. Rohlfs explained. "It features the Battle of Hastings—a subject that has intrigued me since I first learned of the Norman invasion in college. Much of my early poetry, you know, was in the French heroic style. The conqueror-duke from Normandy certainly attracted my interest."

At the time, neither Holmes nor I had attended the exhibit; but given the historical importance of the conflict, we planned to visit the North Hall in the near future. After all, as any British schoolchild could attest, the Battle of Hastings, which marked the victory in 1066 of William, Duke of Normandy, over Harold Godwinson, the last Anglo-Saxon King of England, is generally agreed to have marked the beginnings of modern British society.

"It's really a most thorough presentation," Mrs. Rohlfs reported. "The Hastings exhibition fills the upper-floor galleries on both sides of the central staircase—if you're familiar with the hall."

Now Holmes and I had been to the North Hall many times. Though connected to the main building, it stood to the rear of the Northern Library wing with access only from Montague Place, the museum's northern boundary. The hall had two levels—the ground floor containing meeting rooms and offices and an upper floor where the exhibits were displayed.*

"The northern walls of the upper floor," Mrs. Rohlfs explained, "have numerous paintings of the period as well as a long wall-hanging that depicts the major events of the Battle. On the other side of the stairs there are displays of armour, hauberks, spears, and—"

"—Bows and arrows," injected Holmes as he drew on his pipe.

"Precisely," she said. "Please forgive an American like me for attempting to teach English history to a couple of British gentlemen like yourselves, but weapons are part of my craft. As I'm sure you know, William brought countless Norman

---

* Note that Watson speaks in the past tense. In May 1914, the expansive King Edward VII galleries opened at the northern end of the British Museum, replacing the previous structures in that location.

archers along with him to Hastings. In fact, his bowmen were the first of William's army to set foot on English soil."

Holmes nodded encouragingly, but his rigid jawline told me he was clearly hoping she would move along. For my part, I believed that a discussion of history was Mrs. Rohlfs's way of avoiding the horror she had witnessed earlier in the day.

"For whatever the reason," she said, "whether it was a lack of bowmen in the south or the view that archery was outdated—the English fielded very few archers while the Normans had many."

"Quite," said Holmes impatiently. "But cannot we leap to the end, Mrs. Rohlfs? We know how the battle concludes."

"Almost there, Mr. Holmes," she replied. "Once the English shield-wall fell apart, the Norman arrows found their targets; and—"

"Yes, yes, Mrs. Rohlfs," Sherlock Holmes said sharply, "but it is not the weapons at Hastings with which we are concerned but rather the single arrow let fly today in the museum. Might we not get back to the topic at hand?"

"Of course, Mr. Holmes," Mrs. Rohlfs replied sheepishly. "Forgive me. What would you like to know?"

"Where exactly were you when this tragedy occurred?"

"It was precisely one o'clock," she answered, all business now. "I checked my watch." Here she held up the substantial silver locket hanging round her neck. Opening it revealed a circular clock-face framed in silver. "My father's pocket watch," she explained proudly. "After he died, I had it converted for my own use."

Recalling Holmes's intricate examination of my own watch, I could only imagine what he might be able to deduce about Mrs. Rohlfs's father from the timepiece she had just shown us.

Pointing to the watch for emphasis, Mrs. Rohlfs went on. "I checked to be sure I would have enough time to view the exhibit and still have the chance to meet you gentlemen here for tea as we had planned. All seemed to be in order, and I set about examining a display of swords in a table-length glass case. Norman swords are simple affairs, you know— they are shallow-pointed and have double-edged blades with cross-bars above the hilts to protect the hands. Some were made of iron, but the finer blades were fashioned out of steel."

"And at one o'clock?" Holmes reminded her.

"*You* may find this sword-business irrelevant, Mr. Holmes, but blades fascinate me—all kinds and sizes. I'll have you know that I'm contemplating a novel in which a murder is committed with a hat-pin."*

The woman might have been discussing a dinner menu save for the intensity in her eyes that suggested the cold-blooded seriousness of her plots. She took another sip of the brandy, and her hand was steadier now as she slowly put down the glass.

Holmes puffed sedately on his pipe as he waited for Mrs. Rohlfs to continue. When she failed

---

* *That Affair Next Door* (1897)   The Library of Congress Crime Classics edition is edited by Sherlockian scholar Leslie Klinger, who also contributed an introduction and notes.

to do so, he finally prompted her. "You mentioned that at one o'clock you were looking at swords."

"That is correct," she whispered.

"Well, well," Holmes said, "so you didn't actually see the arrow strike the victim."

"No," replied Mrs. Rohlfs, "not exactly. But I did hear the scream. That's what made me look up. At the same time, someone—an attendant, I learned later—shouted there'd been a terrible accident and to lock the doors. That's when I looked up and saw that beautiful young girl lying on the floor, a feathered arrow protruding from her breast."

"Horrible," I exclaimed.

"A woman standing nearby had rushed to the poor girl's side and crouched over her. In fact, what I first noticed was the woman's hand on the arrow's shaft. I remember thinking how awful it was that she was going to pull the arrow out. But then she let go and frantically called for help.

"Since I was closest to the frightful scene, I steeled myself and rushed over to see what I could do. At first, I thought the woman was whispering into the ear of the dead girl; but in reality, she was sobbing terribly. I laid my hand on her shoulder and whispered that everything would be all right."

"Well done," the doctor inside me observed.

"Within minutes there formed a large, silent circle around the dead girl, the woman holding her, and me trying to comfort the seemingly inconsolable lady. Most of the people had been nearby and came quickly, but there were also a few on the ground-floor—just coming in or going out, I imagine, who drifted up the stairs. You know how people are—

once they become aware that something terrible has happened, they all want to see what's going on."

"One assumes the police were called," Holmes said.

Mrs. Rohlfs nodded. "By that time, the Curator, a wiry old man with a mane of white hair, had come in—Mr. Last, somebody told me his name was. He looked shocked, yet managed to help me get the distraught woman to stand up. He said that when he heard the cry about an accident, he had ordered one of the doormen to summon a constable, and in fact a policeman arrived moments later. It took but a moment for him to size up the situation. He immediately ordered that no one leave and rushed out for help.

"Maybe fifteen minutes later, there appeared an officious little detective—a pale-looking fellow with a sickly pallor who was constantly glancing about. At first, he seemed shifty, but then I could make out the resolve in his eyes. He reminded me of a bird of prey—a hawk or falcon, perhaps."

"Inspector Lestrade," Holmes said, flashing a smile. "A fitting metaphor."

"You forget that I'm a poet as well as a mystery writer, Mr. Holmes.[*] Still, credit where credit is due. It was the man's own intensity that provided the inspiration."

---

[*] See Anna Katharine Green's "The Defence of the Bride," a collection of twenty-six of her poems. Upon reading a selection of Green's poetry, Ralph Waldo Emerson praised her work as revealing "a power of expression" and a "variety and range of . . . thought." Nevertheless, he wisely cautioned her to think carefully about "dar[ing to] leave all other things behind" in order to risk pursuing a career as a poet.

She turned to me. "You're a writer, Doctor. You know what I mean. If memory serves, this same Inspector Lestrade was the detective you wrote about in the Mormon mystery a few years ago—the very person you called a 'sallow rat-faced . . . fellow.'"

My face turned red. It was *A Study in Scarlet* to which she referred. However accurate my description, I find it disconcerting to be rightly accused of depicting someone so critically.

Mrs. Rohlfs took another sip of her brandy. The alcohol seemed to relax her. "Well, Doctor, this time your Inspector Lestrade was on the ball. He'd brought along a half-dozen constables whom he positioned at the stairs and the exit. Once the doors to the street entrance were locked, all of us were effectively confined."

Mrs. Rohlfs was quite right. With the street-doors guarded and the doors to the main building locked, the people in the North Hall had no way out.

"The Curator," she continued, "met the inspector at the top of the stairs. Immediately afterwards, the two were joined by the director of the exhibition, a fellow named Aynesworth."

"Last and Aynesworth," I said. "*The Times* ran a story about the two of them when the Hastings exhibition first opened. If I remember correctly, Anthony Last comes from a wealthy family; he's in his sixties—played football in his youth at Oxford. Supposedly, quite the athlete."

"And the other?" Holmes asked.

"Leonard Aynesworth," I replied, "also wealthy. Lives in Eaton Square. Very good connections. Was married to a baronet's daughter who died last year. Already planning to remarry, the paper said. In fact, he is currently making changes to his house in Eaton Square according to her dictates. The Tories are said to be encouraging him to stand for Parliament."

"Well, I don't know about your Parliament," said Mrs. Rohlfs, "but both men certainly look upper crust. Mr. Last was quite insistent that a thorough investigation be conducted—with discretion, of course. 'We maintain the highest of standards here at the British Museum,' he told Lestrade. In fact, he read word-for-word from a printed directive that listed the proper behaviour for museum officers. He specifically emphasised the charge that museum officials 'conduct themselves as becomes men of honour, integrity and liberality'."

"That hardly settles the matter," Holmes observed.

Mrs. Rohlfs smiled. "I imagine the inspector would agree. He simply touched the brim of his derby and went on with his business. 'The coroner is on his way to examine the body,' he said. 'In the meantime, I want everyone in the building to assemble downstairs.' He then proceeded to order all of us—prospective witnesses I guess you could call us—"

"How many?" Holmes interrupted.

"Twenty-two," she replied. "I counted. None too crowded."

My friend nodded at her preciseness.

"As I was saying, Inspector Lestrade sent everyone down to the foot of the stairs. It took a few minutes for us all to gather there mainly because the woman next to the body—Mrs. Emerald Sommers, I later learned—found it difficult to abandon the dead girl. Only after a constable was posted nearby did she finally agree to allow Mr. Last and me to help her leave the gallery.

"I might add that once she did so, I could see that in spite of her distress, she was quite handsome—well-dressed, well-coiffed, and completely undone by what she had witnessed. I did my best to get her down the stairs, and eventually we joined the others outside the waiting room to see what the police had in store for us."

Chapter Three

The Visitors to the Museum

But hope itself is born of doubt, my friend,
Always in bud, but never quite a flower.
                    --Anna Katharine Green
                    "Hope"

"It was a diverse assortment of people who'd come to observe the Battle of Hastings exhibition that Monday afternoon," Mrs. Rohlfs told us. "As I learned from overhearing Lestrade's questions, the group included a university student writing a thesis on the conflict; an older gentleman fascinated by relics found near the battlefield—pottery, coins, and such; a young woman interested in early British history—she was studying King Harold's victory over an invading Norwegian force at Stamford Bridge in Yorkshire prior to his rush south to Hastings; a pair of newlyweds seeking a quiet place to spend their day together. There was even a young boy, books in hand, working on a project for school."

"Not a murderer among them," I mused.

"And yet, old fellow," Holmes pointed out quite needlessly, "a corpse lay on the museum floor."

Mrs. Rohlfs continued as if we had not quibbled. "The inspector directed each of us to take up the positions we were in when the young woman was struck by the arrow. There was a lot of complaining, I can tell you—everybody wanted to leave. Don't forget that I had an appointment with the two of you here in Baker Street. But the police would hear none of it; and so in spite of the continued griping, we all took our original places, most in the neighbouring galleries of the upper level, a couple on the stairs, and a few near the exit on the ground floor."

"Assuming," observed Holmes, "that everyone took the spot he or she actually occupied at the time of the murder."

"Good point, Mr. Holmes. In any case, the inspector toured the hall, visiting each one of us and making a note of everyone's name and location. Then he herded us all into a large waiting room near the foot of the stairs. There were two rows of benches, enough space to accommodate the entire group."

I knew the room. I myself had spent time in it waiting for Holmes on the occasions when he was late in joining me to view an exhibition.

"Was there an order to your seating?" Holmes asked.

Mrs. Rohlfs pointed a finger of approval in Holmes's direction. "An excellent question. Inspector Lestrade divided us into two groups. He assigned the front benches to those of us who were simply there to visit the exhibit. Those who actually worked in the museum—the two doormen and an attendant as well as the Curator, Mr. Last, and the Director, Mr. Aynesworth—he directed to the back benches.

"Once we were all seated, the inspector began a new list. He asked each of us to repeat our name, furnish our address, explain our business at the museum, and report what we might have observed of the death-scene at the crucial moment.

"Despite one of the constables' standing at the ready to jot down this information in a notebook, it turned out that not a single person—with the notable exceptions of Mrs. Sommers and myself—had any crucial details to report. Inspector Lestrade must have agreed, for once he concluded that he had gotten all the useful information he was going to get from the group, he let the visitors leave."

"Everyone?" Holmes asked.

"Well, not Mrs. Sommers—and not me, I can assure you. Clearly, the inspector had more questions for the woman who'd been found beside the body, and at the same time he also seemed to appreciate the calming effect I had on her. In fact, as Mr. Last and Mr. Aynesworth grew more restless, Inspector Lestrade requested that I remain seated next to Mrs. Sommers while he finished up questioning the museum people."

"Given your late arrival here," Holmes said, pointing his pipe stem at our guest, "you obviously agreed."

"That's right, Mr. Holmes. You see, I felt that I just couldn't abandon the poor woman. So once the inspector motioned for the museum employees to come forward and take their place in the front benches, Mrs. Sommers and I moved to the rear.

"Never a dull moment, however. It was because that area was now empty that I spied a thin strip of black fabric, perhaps two inches long, lying on a square of white tile beneath a back bench. Mind you, I have no sense of what it means or whether it has any connection at all to the business at hand, but at the time it somehow seemed significant."

I was about to enquire why Mrs. Rohlfs thought so, but she anticipated my question.

"Before you ask, gentlemen, I can assure you that, noticeable as it was, I couldn't have missed seeing it had it been lying there when Mrs. Sommers and I originally entered the room. Although we'd been late in joining the group when they were still outside the door, Mrs. Sommers and I were among the first to go in. No black strip had been there then, so help me"—here she raised her right hand as if taking an oath— "so I naturally concluded that one of the museum people who had just been sitting in the back had dropped it."

"Which one?" Holmes asked, his steel-grey eyes glinting as they usually did when he detected possible evidence.

"Hard to say. All five were seated together fairly close together, and each of them walked past where the strip had fallen. Any one of them could have dropped it."

"This black strip," Holmes wanted to know, "what happened to it?"

Smiling broadly, Mrs. Rohlfs reached into her reticule and, withdrawing her closed hand, slowly opened her fingers in front of Holmes. Lying across her palm was the small strip of black cloth she had described. Roughly a half-inch wide and some two to three inches long, it looked like the type of thing one might use to hold an umbrella closed, save that there were no fastening rings at either end.

"Take it," Mrs. Rohlfs said.

Holmes placed his pipe in the glass ashtray next to him and with his long fingers proceeded to snatch the strip from her. He turned the thing over a few times and then, holding it under his lens, pulled from it what appeared to be a strand of white hair.

"Curious," he said and, retrieving a small envelope from the nearby desk, tucked the white hair inside it.

"What good is there in preserving a hair from the floor of the British Museum?" I asked. "It could belong to anyone."

Holmes smiled. "Actually, Watson, it's not a hair, but a barb from a feather—the feather of a swan."

Mrs. Rohlfs furrowed her brow. "Just how does a bit of swan's feather attach itself to a little strip of fabric like that?"

"In due time," Holmes answered with a mysterious smile. Then he looped the strip into a small circle and examined it some more. Moments later, he uncoiled the fabric, slipped it into the envelope with the feather, and moved the collection into his waistcoat pocket.

I knew how my friend operated—when it was time to explain the discovery, he would do so. In the meantime, he resumed asking questions. "What did the museum people have to say for themselves?"

"Not much," the American woman replied. "But I should tell you what else caught my eye. The Curator and the Director wore traditional morning dress—grey cutaway coats with tails, lighter-grey waistcoats, and striped trousers. The others wore their museum uniforms, but the uniforms were of such a middle shade of grey that you might have thought that all five were wearing the same colour. The similarity was underscored by the museum badges pinned to all of their lapels—round, metal affairs with a depiction of the museum's façade engraved on the face."

"Not only do you see, Mrs. Rohlfs," said Holmes, cocking a critical eye in my direction, "but you observe as well. Pray, continue."

"Well, the most interesting among the workers was a young man named Niven Redmond. He's the attendant who raised the alarm. He'd heard the girl's horrific scream when he was going down a narrow stairwell at the rear of the hall. In the few seconds it took for him to reach the ground floor, he had concluded that something was terribly wrong and shouted to lock all the doors."

"Quick thinking," I said.

Holmes simply raised an eyebrow.

"One of the doormen said he'd seen nothing strange, but the other went so far as to admit he was not at his post when Redmond's cry went out to lock the doors. But—"

"Not at his post?" I interrupted. A former military man like myself does not soon forget the dire consequences of such irresponsibility. "If he wasn't in his proper place, might he not have been the villain who shot the arrow?"

"Not hardly," Mrs. Rohlfs smiled, "if you believe his account. He claimed to have rushed back to his position as soon as he heard the command to lock the doors."

"Where was he then?" I asked.

"You'll recall I mentioned a pair of newly-weds? It seems that they were off canoodling in a dark corner, and the doorman, a middle-aged fellow with a strong sense of propriety, boasted of having spotted them. Since the hall wasn't crowded at the time, he left his post in order to end the shocking behaviour. He was following the rules, you see.

"In fact, to defend his actions, he proudly turned to the Curator and the Director who were sitting nearby. 'Such goings-on,' he said to them, 'not supposed to be 'appening in the museum, are they? I went over and put a stop to it. Then I 'ears the call to lock the doors and I rush back to m'post.'

"But the gents who run the place," Mrs. Rohlfs continued, "didn't respond. They seemed more concerned with their own situations than with the heroics of the doorman. The Curator said he was cataloguing a series of medieval paintings in a far-off gallery and arrived at the scene out of breath. And the Director, Aynesworth, said he was near the street exit on the ground floor on his way to another meeting and immediately turned around."

I raised a defiant chin. "Impossible to believe either one of those gentlemen would shoot an arrow into an innocent young girl. Impossible."

Mrs. Rohlfs shrugged. "After Aynesworth had concluded his story, Lestrade dismissed this second group as he had previously excused the museum visitors. Only Mrs. Sommers and I now remained. The inspector stood some distance away and before resuming his interview of Mrs. Sommers reviewed the notes his constable had taken down. If you ask me, when he began questioning her again, he seemed more accusatory than sympathetic."

Holmes nodded at Mrs. Rohlfs's assessment—as if he himself shared her doubts.

"From the way he was slashing his hand down as he spoke to the constable," Mrs. Rohlfs explained, balling her own right hand into a fist and making a swift, downward motion, "I believe he was suggesting that Mrs. Sommers used the arrow like a dagger to stab the poor girl to death—if you can even imagine such a thing."

"A proposition you ruled out?" I asked, "even though you yourself—not to mention all the others— did not actually see the arrow fly."

"Right on both counts, Doctor. But from the position and the suddenness of it all, I just can't see it happening the way Lestrade suggested."

"Quite so," Holmes murmured. "What happened next?"

"When the inspector finished with the constable, he turned towards us. Suddenly, his mouth fell open, and he pointed at Mrs. Sommers.

"So intent had I been on listening to the others tell their stories that I failed to notice the condition of the person sitting right next to me. The poor woman had fainted. Immediately, I began rubbing her hands, and the inspector brought her water. It took a few moments, but even though she moved her head and fluttered her eyelids, she remained groggy."

"Not surprising," I said. "Who wouldn't be upset upon encountering a horror like that—the slaughter of an innocent girl?"

"So true," Mrs. Rohlfs agreed. "In any case, when Mrs. Sommers came around, she murmured something about wanting to go home.

"The inspector was not finished with her, however. 'A few more questions,' he countered. 'Then we'll be done—for now. Once more, describe what you saw.'

"The woman took a deep breath and sat up straight. 'I've already told you,' she said, her voice full of exasperation. 'I was walking through the gallery towards the railing at the stairs when the girl stepped in front of me, and I saw her stagger backward into the gallery and fall. What else was there to do but rush to her side? That's when I saw the arrow in her breast.' She shook her head. 'It was horrible.'

"'You didn't observe it in flight then?' Lestrade asked. 'Or hear it fly past?'

"'No,' she whispered.

"Curious," Holmes noted. "Neither one of you ladies saw the arrow fly."

"Correct," Mrs. Rohlfs said. "But the inspector had an explanation. 'Perhaps you didn't see it or hear it,' he said to Mrs. Sommers with an edge to his voice, 'because it never did fly past. Perhaps what did happen is that you grabbed an arrow from the display next to you and for whatever your deranged reason, you stabbed the young woman to death with a single blow.'

"Mrs. Sommers shook her head. 'No, no—that didn't happen. I never saw the girl before today. Why would I do such a thing?'

"Lestrade radiated confidence when he announced, 'A witness'—that would be me, gentlemen," added Mrs. Rohlfs— "'reported that you had your hand on the arrow. Most incriminating, wouldn't you say?'

"Mrs. Sommers shook her head in denial. 'I thought to withdraw the arrow, but then I worried that pulling it out might kill her—if somehow she wasn't dead already.'

"Lestrade arched his eyebrows in disbelief. 'Let us try another approach, Mrs. Sommers. You said you were heading towards the railing. Was it to see the collection on the other side of the stairs?'

"'No, I—I was just looking out over the court.'

"'And you say you saw no one on the opposite side—no one in the galleries across the stairs?'

"She ran her hands through her hair. 'No, I tell you. It was all such a shock. It's something I'll never forget as long as I live.' As we pondered the truth of that answer, I asked the inspector if I might pose a question of my own.

"'Let's hear it,' he said.

"'Mrs. Sommers,' I asked, 'are you interested in the Battle of Hastings? Is that what brought you here today?'"

"Excellent, Mrs. Rohlfs," Holmes observed. "How did she answer?"

"'No.' She said, 'no.' She explained that she was just passing through the building.

"With that response, the inspector seemed to have had enough. 'All right then, Mrs. Sommers,' he said, 'we'll let you go for the present. I'll get a constable to take you to your rooms.'

"'No police,' Mrs. Sommers said firmly. 'I'll find a cab.'

"'Suit yourself,' Lestrade shrugged. But before letting her leave, he added, 'You understand that you must remain available to us for further questioning.'

"Mrs. Sommers nodded silently, and I helped the poor woman to her feet. 'I'll ride along with you,' I offered as I escorted her out of the museum and into Montague Place.

"Mrs. Sommers shook her head. 'Thank you, but I'd like to be alone. I've been through a lot today.'

"'You're certain you're okay?'

"She nodded, and we searched in vain for a hansom."

"Cabs are forever hovering about the main entrance to the Museum in Great Russell Street," I noted. "Not so often in Montague Place."

"Right you are, Doctor," said Mrs. Rohlfs. "We hurried over to the next corner—"

"Montague Street," I said, recalling that it was home to the first flat in London occupied by Sherlock Holmes.

"—turned right and made our way to the front of the museum. There was a queue already formed."

"The British Museum stays open late on Monday evenings during the summer," I explained.

"Well, we waited our turn. Finally, Mrs. Sommers was able to climb into a hansom. 'The Medallion Hotel,' I heard her shout up to the driver, a distinctive fellow with a top hat and long red beard. Immediately, they clattered off down the road. I took the next cab and came here to Baker Street for our meeting—hours late, as it turned out."

"Now that you're here," I said, "I'm sure that Mrs. Hudson could muster dinner for the three of us."

Mrs. Rohlfs raised her hand to stop me. "Thank you," she said, "but I have my family back at Brown's. It's high time I join them."

With promises exchanged to share any new facts concerning the terrible death at the museum, Mrs. Rohlfs pulled on her gloves. When we reached the stairs, however, both of us caught sight of Mrs. Hudson.

More accurately, we caught sight of Mrs. Hudson about to lead a uniformed policeman up to Holmes's door. As they approached us on the stairs, Mrs. Rohlfs turned her face towards the wall and allowed them to pass. Upon reaching the ground floor, she whispered to me, "He was one of the officers at the museum this afternoon. I thought it better that he not know I was here."

When I returned to Holmes's rooms, I found him reading a note the constable had delivered. After a moment, he handed it to me. "*Bizarre murder at*

British Museum. Hastings exhibit. North Hall. Come immediately." It was signed. "*G. Lestrade.*"

"Perfect timing, eh, Watson?" Holmes said.

"There's a van outside, Mr. Holmes," the constable offered.

"What say you?" Holmes asked me. "Interested in a case at the British Museum? The game's afoot, after all."

"Indeed," I answered. I was about to add, "Especially in light of the provocative account we've already heard"; but looking at the constable, I thought it better to hold my tongue than to admit we had just been entertaining one of Lestrade's own witnesses.

Holmes and I reached for our coats and followed the policeman down the stairs. A growler pulled by two high-stepping black horses awaited, and a short drive along the Marylebone Road and then along Gower Street, brought us to our destination.

Chapter Four

A Witness to Murder

If . . . there is some mystery about the motive,
or about the act itself, we follow every detail of the case
with what is commonly called "morbid curiosity."
--Anna Katharine Green
"Why Human Beings are
Interested in Crime"
American Magazine
1919

*P*eople familiar with London are well acquainted with the grand entrance to the British Museum. Set in Great Russell Street, it features a classical, colonnaded portico surmounted by a pediment of allegorical figures that champion the progress of civilisation. Yet in the darkening twilight, the police van drove quickly past the celebrated façade and round the historic building via Bloomsbury Street to Montague Place and the museum's less-trafficked rear entrance.

The North Hall's portal, which was accessed from the road, appeared much less imposing than the dramatic frontage in Great Russell Street. Still, it featured a perfectly serviceable set of concrete stairs which led the visitor to the large hall so highly regarded at the time for its ever-changing dramatic exhibitions.

Informed of our impending arrival, the constables who were standing guard at the entrance allowed us to pass. The familiar smell of history—a melange of dry wood, worn leather, and antiquated metals—greeted us as soon as we entered. The shockingly bright illumination that bathed every recess, however, was a new development.

To be sure, the British Museum was one of the first public buildings in London to install electric lighting, yet the intent was never to outperform the powers of Helios himself. Clearly, in order to aid their current investigation, the police were taking full advantage of the modernisation. All the globes were ablaze.

With the nod of his head, Holmes indicated the two constables posted by the mahogany-balustrade at the top of the grand marble staircase. They marked our obvious destination. Before we could begin our climb, however, Inspector Lestrade intercepted us.

"Thought you might be interested in this grotesque affair, Mr. Holmes," he said with a sardonic smile.

Unaware of the facts made known to us earlier by Mrs. Rohlfs, Lestrade pushed back the bowler he constantly wore and went on to recount the key elements related to the crime—the death of the poor young woman struck by an arrow, the interrogation of the people in the hall at the time, the woman about whom he had expressed his suspicions.

"A most interesting puzzle," Holmes agreed.

"I reckoned you'd see it that way," said Lestrade, folding his arms across his chest, "though I fear I may not need your help after all. I do think the problem may already be solved."

"How so?" Holmes asked.

The inspector pointed at a nearby room. Through its open door, one could see two rows of benches. "That's where we put the people who were here when the poor girl was killed. There were a number of them."

"Twenty-two," I blurted out.

Though it was I who had uttered the words, Lestrade narrowed his dark eyes at Holmes as well as me. "How do you know the precise number then?" he asked warily.

It was clear that I had spoken too quickly.

"An estimate from the number of benches," Holmes improvised. Obviously, he too had no desire to publicise Mrs. Rohlfs's involvement.

Lestrade looked unconvinced. "In any case," said he, "we interviewed them all, got their names and addresses, and sent them packing. Against my better judgement, I also allowed the woman we found huddling over the body to return to her rooms in the Medallion. It's a family hotel in High Holborn, and she's lived there for a number of months. Mrs. Emerald Sommers, she calls herself, and she appears very shaken by all that's happened—very shaken indeed. So much so, let me say, that she has raised my suspicions."

"Explain your reasoning," said Holmes.

The inspector grinned. In the unforgiving glare of the bright electric lighting, his yellow teeth looked particularly feral.

"In the first place, Mr. Holmes, let me assure you that we've had no reports of anyone trying to escape from the building. Thus, we are concentrating all our efforts on what was going on within."

"Quite reasonable," Holmes said.

"As yet, my men have found no bow that might have been employed in this frightful deed or received the slightest word of anyone seen carrying such a weapon. Nor are there any arrows exhibited on the upper floor's northern side from where, one must presume, the deadly arrow would have been shot.

"On the other hand, a large quiver was standing upright on the floor within the reach of Mrs. Sommers. According to the Curator, it originally contained"—here Lestrade consulted his notes— "eleven arrows. After the murder, we counted; there were only ten—now, actually, only nine since I brought one down here for a closer look myself." He picked up the arrow that was lying on a nearby table and handed it to Holmes.

"Norman," Holmes muttered, which made sense since, as Mrs. Rohlfs had reminded us, Norman archers dominated the battlefield. Sighting down the shaft, he pronounced, "Willow," and running his fingers along the length, particularly over the fletching, observed, "Swan—as I suspected."

With great care, Holmes then touched his forefinger to the sharp, elongated point of the arrowhead, a black, metal-squared spike.

"A bodkin arrowhead," Holmes informed us. "It can pierce chainmail and shatter bone like a bullet. One shudders to think what it did to that poor girl." Laying the arrow back on the table, Holmes asked, "Now what about its delivery? What of the bows in the exhibit?"

Lestrade crossed his arms in front of his chest. "As I've already told you, Mr. Holmes, we've found no bow that connects to this crime. All twelve on display remain mounted on a wall on the south side of the upper floor. I do have to say that they're amazingly small."

"Not surprising," Holmes nodded. "Although the Normans certainly had long bows, many others, like this one, were only about twenty inches in length. But don't let that fool you. These smaller bows were made from strong yew, strung with resilient hemp, and in the right hands could hit a target at one-hundred yards."

Lestrade's eyes widened at this information—or perhaps at the fact that Holmes possessed it so readily. "Be that as it may, Mr. Holmes, I'm sure you'll agree that—bow or no bow—it was clearly the arrow which was responsible for the crime. The woman, Mrs. Sommers, was seen to have had her hand on the shaft that had pierced the dead girl's body. Since no bow has turned up, it seems more than reasonable to conclude that Mrs. Sommers stabbed the girl with the arrow. All I lack is a motive."

Holmes and I exchanged sceptical glances.

"Oh, I know you private detectives have your own methods," Lestrade proceeded, "I'll give you that. A few of your results have even helped me out a bit. I'd be much obliged if you can use some of your skill to determine why this woman would stab to death so beautiful a young girl."

"Surely, you have some ideas of your own, Lestrade," replied Holmes. "What do *you* believe the motive to have been?"

The policeman stroked his chin and furrowed his brow, sure signs that he was trying to think. At last, he said, "With the woman's great confusion and distress—she fainted, don't you know, right in her chair—brain fever seems the obvious explanation. Until I hear otherwise, I will continue to believe that a deranged person—this Emerald Sommers— plucked an arrow from an available quiver and stabbed a lovely young girl to death without any explanation whatsoever. Sheer madness."

"Perhaps," Holmes said. "In any case, I need to view the body before additional time goes by and the scene of the crime becomes even more corrupted."

"Right you are, Mr. Holmes," Lestrade agreed, and we all made our way up the grand stairs and onto the walkway that encircled the stairwell, turning left towards the southern side of the hall. A series of open galleries, each linked to its neighbours through connecting archways, faced the walkway. In single file, we marched to the near-centre of the passage to the gallery entrance guarded by a constable.

As a physician not unfamiliar with death, I still find it difficult to describe the horrific scene: Beneath the singularly bright electric lamps, the black and white squares of the floor at the front of the gallery looked like a draughts-board—save that upon its cold, chequered tiles lay the lifeless body of a young girl no older than sixteen or seventeen. She was lying on her back, and the long, navy-blue police coat in which she was shrouded did nothing to disguise the tell-tale protuberance responsible for the grisly murder.

Gently, Lestrade pulled away the covering, and one could surmise from the styled cut of the poor creature's flaxen hair and the quality of her pleated, white shirtwaist and charcoal skirt that she came from a genteel background, perhaps the daughter of a merchant or professional.

Her eyes were closed, and a round white hat lay beneath her blond curls. White gloves graced her small hands. She might have been asleep save for the trail of blood that had dripped down her side from the wound in her breast and pooled in an oval beneath her—that, and the arrow's stark shaft with its white feathers projecting heavenward some eighteen inches above the lethal wound.

There was no practical need for a doctor to examine the victim, not with that upright arrow so prominent. If truth be told, as I knelt over the body, I could not escape contemplating the irony of so disheartening a tragedy. Before me lay the remains of a murdered young innocent in a particularly grand museum, an institution whose pediment gracing its Great Russell Street entrance champions the progress of human civilization. The progress of human civilization indeed!

I backed away slowly from the dead girl and allowed Holmes to move in. Armed with his magnifying lens, he circled the body, staring down at the floor as he did so.

"No purse, Lestrade?" he asked without looking up.

"A small, white-beaded affair," the inspector answered. "It was lying by her side, and we picked it up. Nothing to identify her, just some coins and a tiny, blank notebook. One of my men will give it to the coroner when he gets here."

Holmes responded with an exasperated shake of his head. Then he dropped to his knees to scrutinise the wound and the angle of the arrow that caused it. A few moments later, he stood up and stared at the galleries on the other side of the stairs.

"What are you looking for?" Lestrade questioned.

"The arrow came in at too low an angle for the wound to be made as you suggest. There is no indication of severe downward thrust. No," he said, pointing across the stairwell, "it had to have come from over there."

Lestrade opened his mouth, presumably to argue, but immediately closed it without saying a word.

"Keep the exhibit closed tomorrow," Holmes said. "I'd very much like to come back and study the lie of the land."

"Exactly our intention," Lestrade nodded and carefully began re-settling the long coat over the dead girl. As he did so, a young man in a dark-grey museum uniform approached him.

"What is it?" Lestrade grumbled. "Who the devil are you?"

"Niven Redmond, sir," the young man answered, casting a nervous glance at the now-covered body.

Holmes stared at the fellow. In Baker Street, Mrs. Rohlfs had reported that it was this same Niven Redmond who had cried out to lock all the doors.

"I work here," Redmond reminded Lestrade. "I'm an attendant; you—you questioned me earlier."

Nettled at having forgotten the witness, Lestrade barked, "What do you want then?"

Before Redmond could answer, my friend interrupted. "My name is Sherlock Holmes," he said to the attendant, "and I am a detective. Would you be good enough to let me examine your jacket?"

Lestrade's eyes widened in surprise. "Here now, Mr. Holmes, what's this about then?"

"Testing a theory, Lestrade. Have patience."

The policeman removed his bowler and scratched his head though I, having seen Holmes roll the strip into a circle, believed his request made sense.

If one assumed that the bit of feather embedded in the strip of fabric Mrs. Rohlfs had found had come from an arrow's fletching, could one not imagine the strip in circular form sewn into the lining of a coat or jacket? As such, it would provide within the coat a concealed loop from which the murderer could hang the fatal arrow whilst transporting it unseen from where it was displayed on one side of the hall to where it would be employed for deadly purpose on the other.

If the killer had been among those whom Lestrade had interrogated earlier in the day, the danger of being found out might well have prompted the culprit to secretly tear the loop from its sticking place and discard it on the floor prior to facing the inspector. Find the tell-tale coat, and discover the identity of the killer—provided the villain had not already destroyed the incriminating garment.

With Nevin Redmond still in uniform now standing before us, it seemed quite logical that Holmes would want to inspect the young man's jacket.

"Happy to cooperate," Niven said in response to Holmes's request, "but I assure you that I have something to show you that will interest you more."

None the less, Holmes gestured that the attendant remove his jacket; and brushing a shock of dark hair from his eyes, the young man complied.

Sherlock Holmes held up the dark jacket, scrutinised its front and back, and peered along the sleeves. Only then did he open it wide and examine the light-grey lining. Upon finding nothing of interest, he returned it to the attendant.

"I'm telling you, gentlemen," Niven said as he shrugged on his jacket, "I found evidence I'm certain that you'll want to see. Please, follow me."

With Niven's credibility having already been established for us by Mrs. Rohlfs, Holmes, and I were quick to fall in line; and Lestrade muttering,

"Evidence, is it?" trailed after us. We marched round the stairs to the northern side of the hall and followed the young man into the gallery whose wide rear-wall featured the historical tapestry.

I should also add that at either end of the wall-hanging—that is, in both rear corners of the gallery some thirty feet apart—stood large, white pedestals—four-foot cubes, actually—upon each of which rested an even larger dark-green, ceramic vase or urn.

The bulky corner-displays suggested that Niven might have discovered some sort of hiding place employed by the killer; but the attendant, moved past the urn closest to us, stopping instead at the left-hand corner of the tapestry.

"Behold, gentlemen," he announced as he drew back the lower section of the stiff fabric.

The tapestry had been mounted a foot away from the wall, and enough area was now exposed to reveal a small, black door. And yet it was not this hidden door that highlighted Niven's revelation; it was the object leaning against the left-side doorjamb to which he pointed. There, in the shadows of the niche, stood a short, wooden bow. Unlike its fellows on display in the other side of the hall, this one most certainly was well strung.

Lestrade let out a long, slow whistle.

"I remembered the door and happened to look behind the tapestry," Niven explained, "and there it was."

Holmes took a step forward. "If we assume that the bow in front of us is the one that shot the deadly arrow, I think we may safely cast aside the theory that the young lady was stabbed to death by an arrow wielded like a knife. Would you not agree, Lestrade?"

The inspector shifted from one foot to the other. "I suppose so," he finally admitted. "This really does change everything."

Holmes picked up the bow and turned to the attendant. "Any idea how this got here, Niven?" he asked, handing it to him. "Have a closer look."

The young man took the bow from Holmes and slowly rolled it in his fingers. As he did so, he used his thumb to massage a section a few inches from the top. A moment later, he brought the shaft closer to his eyes and examined the area more carefully.

At last, he said, "I do believe that I *have* seen this bow before—I mean before tonight. I recall this nick." He pointed to a small, white notch near the top of the upper limb.

Holmes noted it as well.

"The bow was removed from the exhibit," Niven said, "because the nick was too recent—I mean, not from the eleventh century, not made during the Battle of Hastings. The historians could tell—something about the light colour of the exposed wood. There were enough other Norman bows in better shape, so they didn't need this one."

"Where do you remember first seeing it?" Holmes asked.

Niven furrowed his brow. "I believe it was lying in an open storage case in the cellar beneath the Curator's office. It's where they store the artifacts they feel shouldn't be on display."

"Like a bow with a modern notch in it," I said.

"Yes, sir," replied Niven.

"Who has access to the cellar?" Lestrade wanted to know.

Niven furrowed his brow again. I imagine he realised the implication of his answer. "The cellar is open only to people who work here—certainly, not to the public."

"Only the people who work here," Lestrade smiled. "Limits the suspects, eh, Mr. Holmes?"

"Perhaps," said my friend.

The inspector pursed his lips, but Holmes had more questions for the attendant. "What about this doorway itself? Could someone have brought the bow through it?"

"I doubt it, Mr. Holmes. The door is always locked; and to the best of my knowledge, the stairs haven't been used in years. That's why it took me a while to remember it. The stairway itself leads down to the Curator's office. As far as I know, no one comes in this way."

"Who has the key?" Lestrade asked.

"Why, Mr. Last, the Curator. It's on a hook near his desk."

"Available to anyone who might find himself in the Curator's office then," observed the inspector.

Niven simply shrugged.

Lestrade reached out his hand and reclaimed the bow. "Well done, lad," he said with a begrudging smile. Offering a note of finality, he added, "We have your address, so we know how to find you." Then he sent the young man on his way.

Moments later, Holmes and I were following Lestrade down the stairs. At the table upon which lay the Norman arrow, the inspector set down the bow.

Suddenly, a cry rang out. "Hoi! Stop!"

In the silence of the empty hall, we could hear the clatter of footfalls echoing overhead, and immediately we looked up. Across the brightly lit upper floor a figure was dashing along the corridor towards the central staircase, the constable who had shouted at him in hot pursuit.

It was another policeman at the top of the stairs, however, who grasped the fugitive by his shoulders. As soon as the fellow was accosted, he crumpled to the floor. The constable laid an authoritative knee upon the man's back to keep him from attempting any other means of escape.

Chapter Five

A New Suspect

No matter how carefully a crime may be planned,
or covered up, the criminal almost invariably
forgets some significant detail.
--Anna Katharine Green
"Why Human Beings are
Interested in Crime"
American Magazine, 1919

"*B*ring that man down here!" Lestrade shouted.

The constable jerked the fellow to his feet and steered him roughly down the stairs. Once they reached the ground floor, the policeman shoved him into a chair before the inspector.

A smartly dressed but winded young man sat before us. Inhaling deeply and desperately trying to catch his breath, he did not raise his head.

"Popped out from behind one of those great pots, he did," reported the policeman. "Simmons hailed him, and he run straight into me arms."

"Well, well, Lestrade," Holmes said, "it would appear that you have an additional suspect." I could hear the ripple of satisfaction in my friend's voice even if the inspector could not.

For his part, the poor fellow sat head in hands beneath the unrelenting lights.

"Here now," Lestrade demanded, "What's your name?"

"Andrew Stanford," came the answer between deep breaths. He spoke with an American accent.

Oddly distrait, the man refrained from looking any of us in the eye, yet the family name sounded familiar. For an instant, I thought of our old friend *Stamford*, who had introduced me to Sherlock Holmes back in '81; but with the American pronunciation and the quality of the man's clothes, I was reminded of the Stanford connected to the railway industry in the United States.

Lestrade identified Holmes and me and then began his questions. "Mr. Stanford," he said, "we're in need of an explanation. What were you doing hiding upstairs? I should imagine you've been there since that young girl was murdered."

At the reference to the poor victim, the man's eyes welled with tears. "I was enchanted by her," he confessed. "I first saw her on the boat from Calais. I'm touring Europe, you see—a gift from pater to celebrate my graduation from college—Yale, that is. I'd been in France; and aboard the ship to Dover, I couldn't keep my eyes off her. Blonde. Smiling. Classic profile. Altogether charming."

Lestrade appeared unconvinced; I, on the other hand, found young Stanford's explanation rather moving.

"Remember your Shakespeare, inspector?" Stanford asked. "'Whoever loved that loved not at first sight?' That's me."

"Originally, Marlowe," Holmes commented. "Later appropriated by Shakespeare."

For a man whose knowledge of literature I had once labelled as "nil," the scope of Holmes's learning never failed to amaze me. Still, whether credit for the observation belonged to Marlowe or to Shakespeare, the young man seemed a romantic at heart, and I was sympathetic.

After all, I had been smitten in much the same fashion. As I have written elsewhere, I will never forget my first view of Mary's amiable face, a sweet visage that revealed her refined and sensitive nature. Many are the nights that I still fall asleep beneath its loving if illusory gaze.

Lestrade's voice broke into my reverie. "Explain," he directed Stanford.

The young man looked up. "By nature, I—I am a timid fellow; and she was traveling with an extremely protective lady, whom though darker in complexion and possessing a drooping left eyelid I took to be her mother. At the very least, the woman kept the girl at a distance from me. None the less, I stayed close when we docked in Dover, and I managed to occupy a nearby seat in the train to Victoria."

"Surely, the young lady noticed you?" my romantic self asked.

The young man smiled wistfully. "We exchanged glances, so I know she saw me. But nothing more."

"And once here in London?" Holmes pressed.

"At Victoria, I overheard her mother in a decidedly French accent tell the hansom driver to take them to Brown's Hotel. I hailed a cab and followed. After all, I'd been struck by Cupid's arrow."

Holmes, Lestrade and I exchanged surprised looks at Stanford's misguided allusion.

"Oh, sorry," he blushed, realizing his lack of sensitivity, "a bad choice of words. In any case, Brown's had a room available; and with the allowance I get from pater, I could easily afford to take it. As soon as I had finished registering, I planted myself in the lobby and waited for the girl to make an appearance."

Holmes leaned forward. "You said the two women were staying at Brown's. Did you get their names?"

Stanford shook his head.

"Hard to believe," I said, "a young man as love-struck as yourself and you didn't survey the names when you registered."

"Alas, no," he groaned. "I was given a fresh page in the book to sign."

"You mean to say," I replied in disbelief, "that you couldn't think of a way to procure the name of this young woman, your newly discovered *inamorata*?"

The young man shook his head again, a silent admission of his feckless wooing.

"And you did not speak to them in the hotel?" I persisted.

Andrew Stanford hung his head. "I already told you, gentlemen. I'm shy, especially around women. It's tough to admit, but there you have it."

Silence followed as we three questioners pondered what to ask this unimaginative American.

"Watson," Holmes said at last, "our visitor at Baker Street this afternoon said she was returning to Brown's. Perhaps we can make use of her detecting skills. One cannot deny that she's shown some promise."

"Who's this then?" Lestrade wanted to know.

"A person of interest," Holmes answered simply as he withdrew a small pocket-book from inside his coat and tore out a single page. He proceeded to write a few words on it. I could not help noticing that after folding the paper, he printed "Anna Katharine Green" on the outside rather than the woman's married name, which Lestrade might possibly have recognised among those of his witnesses earlier that afternoon.

"May I employ one of your constables, Lestrade?" Holmes asked, holding up the paper. "If all goes well, your man should be back within the half-hour."

"I suppose so," Lestrade frowned and beckoned a constable with a wave.

"For Miss Green at Brown's Hotel," Holmes advised, handing the policeman the note. "Wait for a reply."

The constable offered an informal salute and marched off.

All the while, Andrew Stanford sat slowly rocking back and forth in his chair. He presented so despairing a figure, one wondered why he thought an attractive young woman like the poor girl who had been killed that day might have taken an interest in him.

Even I, the most sympathetic of his interrogators, could not understand what had prevented the fellow from approaching mother and daughter and introducing himself. After all, he had admitted to us that he came from a well-to-do family; and grief aside, he appeared presentable enough. But then love can handicap its most intense purveyors.

Holmes's interest in Stanford's psychology was more practical. "How do you balance your timidity," Holmes asked the fellow, "with your pursuit of the young woman here to the museum? A timid person would not be inclined to follow."

Stanford raised his head. "Actually, since you raise the question, there was a degree of concern that prompted me."

Holmes leaned in again. "How so?"

A spark of light suddenly shone in Stanford's eyes. He seemed to have discovered that he possessed some useful information. "I've already described how I was sitting in the hotel lobby. Within the hour, the young lady and her mother came down the stairs together, but only the young woman was dressed to go out."

"In what sense?" asked Holmes.

"She wore a white shirtwaist and dark skirt along with a hat, and gloves—quite beautiful, as I have said." He smiled at the memory. "Her mother, however, was dressed in the same dark clothing she'd been wearing on the boat, and her hair had not been fixed."

"Curious," said Holmes.

"But there's more, gentlemen. Her mother looked worried—distressed really. She spoke to the girl in French—" here the young man placed a humble hand to his chest— *"mais je parle français. I heard her explain to the girl that she, her mother, was not allowed to go with her."*

"Not *allowed*?" I repeated.

"Yes— *'interdit'* was the word she used. I tell you, gentlemen, it was just such a comment, along with the mother's obvious worry, that caused me unease. It may sound silly—I mean, I didn't know either of them—but somehow, I wondered if the young lady might be in some sort of danger."

"A leap at the time," I observed, "but quite prescient in terms of the horror that transpired."

Lestrade folded his arms and exhaled loudly, yet Stanford seemed to miss the inspector's scepticism.

"I remember thinking," Stanford said, "that maybe I could be of help to her."

"Some sort of new-found gallantry," I suggested.

"I suppose so, Doctor, now that you mention it. In any case, I decided to listen for her destination. It was here, as it turned out—the North Hall of the British Museum, and I hired a cab of my own to follow hers. We arrived just moments apart.

"I was careful to keep out of sight as I trailed after her, and once inside I watched her climb the stairs. She turned left at the top, and I turned right, for it was my intention to observe her in secret from the other side of the hall. The gallery with the tapestry was the perfect spot."

"More cowardly than timid," Lestrade muttered.

Holmes surveyed both sides of the upper floor. "Let's retrace Stanford's route, Lestrade," he said and, without waiting for a reply, motioned for the young man to conduct us to his hidey-hole.

Stanford led us up the stairs and, turning to the northern side, proceeded down the open corridor to the gallery containing the tapestry. Pointing to the right, he said, "I squeezed in behind that green urn in the corner."

"'Hid' is more like it," grumbled Lestrade as Stanford directed Holmes into the tight fit between the pedestal supporting the urn and the back-wall.

"That's exactly where I was when I saw her approach the railing," said Stanford. "I remember thinking that maybe she saw me come up here and, free of her mother, wanted to get my attention."

"It's quite a good spot," Holmes said. "One doesn't have to expose one's head back here. There's quite a clear view through the space between the wall and the wide curve at the bottom of the urn. You can see across the stairs and into the gallery where the arrow struck." He paused a moment, before reporting, "Right now, in fact, I can see the coroner removing the body."

We all turned, and Holmes extricated himself from Stanford's hiding place. An aging official was just then directing a pair of men clad in black to place the poor girl's body on a stretcher and carry her down the stairs. Two others cleaned up the mess on the floor, and a constable handed the coroner the small white purse to which Lestrade had referred earlier. The four of us stood by quietly until the procession had passed out of the building.

Once the sombre march ended, Holmes asked Stanford, "What did you see when you were behind the urn?"

"I watched her enter the first gallery over there and walk through the neighbouring rooms until she finally came running towards the balustrade."

"Can you describe the angle she took?" Holmes asked

"I'm not sure. I know she entered from the archway of the adjacent room, and she moved past a woman towards the rail. The next thing I knew, the arrow had struck."

"From where did it come?" Lestrade demanded.

"I don't know," Stanford whispered. "From this side of the stairs, I'm sure. But I didn't see anyone shoot it. Once I got in between the wall and the urn, I remember glancing around the gallery—to be certain no one had noticed me sneak into my hiding place. After I heard the cry, I looked back across the way and saw the arrow in her breast and the stricken girl in the arms of the lady she had run by. I was devastated."

I laid a hand on the poor fellow's shoulder as his head sank down.

"One last request, Stanford," said Sherlock Holmes. "With Dr. Watson's permission, I'm going to send him across the way. When he reaches the spot where the young lady stood at the time she was struck, I'd like you to tell me."

From one of his many pockets, Holmes produced a piece of chalk, which he handed to me; I then hastened round the head of the stairs to the other side of the building.

I entered the gallery next to the murder scene and proceeded through the archway Stanford had indicated. Despite the clean-up work of the coroner's men, a dull, reddish shadow remained on the chequer-board floor.

Avoiding the stains, I approached the balustrade in what I hoped was the same angle Stanford had described. I then began turning in the direction of the men across the way, looking for a signal to stop. When I was almost directly facing the railing, I saw Stanford touch Holmes's arm, and Holmes put up his hand to alert me. I bent over and chalked the outline of my boots on the floor.

My job completed, I made my way back to the other side of the hall. As it turned out, the constable Holmes had sent with the message for Anna Green was returning at the same time.

"Our friend at Brown's has responded," Holmes announced upon opening the note the policeman handed him. "The French woman is called Madame Marie Costerd. Her daughter—that is to say, the tragic victim, Angelique Costerd."

"Angelique," murmured Andrew Stanford. "She was indeed an angel, and I could do nothing to protect her." Standing up straighter now, he addressed Lestrade. "You'll find the person who did this, Inspector. I won't leave London until the monster who shot that arrow is discovered."

"At Scotland Yard we always get our man, Mr. Stanford. Don't you worry about that." Lestrade turned to my friend. "Now then, Mr. Holmes, any last questions for this gentleman? Any concerns about his jacket, for instance?"

"No, Lestrade. Unlike those to whom you spoke in your initial round of interviews, Stanford here never entered the room where you placed the witnesses. For that matter, having just arrived in London on the day of the murder, he would have had no opportunity either to set up a hiding place for the bow or to secure the arrow. It is safe to say that you may exclude this fellow from your list of suspects."

"Not that I follow your logic," Lestrade said, "but until we catch the murderer, I will not exclude Mr. Stanford—or anyone else, for that matter—from suspicion." Only after jotting in his pocket-book that Stanford was staying at Brown's did he finally let the poor fellow go.

"We plan on continuing this investigation tomorrow morning, Mr. Holmes," the inspector added. "The exhibition will remain closed until we are satisfied that we haven't missed anything. We begin at 9.00."

"With Dr. Watson's agreement, the two of us shall be here as well."

Needless to say, I nodded confirmation.

Lestrade offered to drive us back to Baker Street, but Holmes and I chose to walk.

"Early tomorrow morning," Holmes said to me as we were descending the stairs, "I must post a telegram."

Pondering where such a telegram might be sent, I happened to look back at the tapestry. In some sort of historical irony, the crewelwork embroidery in the section behind which we had found the bow depicted the grim, legendary fate of the last of the Anglo-Saxon kings. During the Battle of Hastings, Harold Godwinson was shot dead, his eye said to have been penetrated by a well-directed Norman arrow.

Chapter Six

Reconstructing the Crime

The world means more to the artist than to other people,
for he is constantly following out the delicate threads of
thought, feeling, and action, tangling and untangling them . . .
searching for the secret heart of all.

--Anna Katharine Green
Letter to friend and writer
Mary Hatch
August 22, 1880

I paused on the staircase when I came down
for breakfast the next morning, for I was surprised to
see a bald-headed stranger sitting at our table—
perhaps, I mused, the mysterious recipient of
Holmes's telegram. I could not be certain, however,
for not only was the person's back turned to me; but
I had just awakened, and my vision was none too
sharp.

"Who—?" I asked as I proceeded down the
stairs.

Holmes greeted me with a dry laugh. "From
my closet full of tricks, old fellow. You know my
methods."

I did, indeed. To my great chagrin, I quickly
discovered that there was no guest at table at all, but
rather a life-sized, flesh-coloured mannequin dressed

in white shirt and black trousers lacking any sense of recognizable facial features.

There was nothing to be said in response, so I immediately sat down and poured myself a cup of coffee.

"This fellow," Holmes pointed a butter knife at the mannequin, "will help reveal the nature of the murder at the museum, but I shall leave it to Langdon Steeples, one of the Cambridge Bowmen, to confirm it. I sent him a telegram this morning."

"Langdon Steeples," I repeated. From the Lord St. Sylvester case the year before, I recognised the name—a reputed master with the bow and arrow. I had not actually met the man; but I knew he had instructed Holmes in archery, so my friend could compete in His Lordship's shooting contest with a business magnate suspected of murder.

"I didn't tell you of Steeples last night because I wanted to be certain he could meet us at the Hastings exhibit. In fact, he will be at the North Hall later this morning."

I nodded approval and began my breakfast. I was finishing the kedgeree and Holmes his coffee when a knock rattled the door.

"Enter," Holmes called, and Billy the page strode in. "Mrs. Charles Rohlfs," he announced, and in marched our visitor from the previous day, dressed on this occasion in a dark-brown dress with white trimming and old-fashioned, floral-patterned embroidery on the front.

Holmes and I both rose and donned our jackets.

"Good morning, gentlemen," she said. "I don't have much time since Charles and I are taking the children to Hamley's Toys in High Holborn." Noticing the dummy, she arched an eyebrow. "You, I see, have no need for new toys."

"Helping with our investigation," I tried to explain.

Mrs. Rohlfs waved away my comment. "I have some additional information to share," she announced. "It regards the women you asked about last night."

"Do tell," said Holmes, gesturing in the direction of the basket-chair.

"No time to sit," she said quickly. "After securing the names of the two women, I thought I might try some investigating on my own. I mean, the police hadn't arrived at the hotel yet, so why not? 'What would my fictional Inspector Gryce want to know?' I asked myself."

"And the answer?" Holmes prompted.

"I told the clerk I wanted to visit the two women in question and asked for their room number. He gave it to me, but in looking up the details discovered that in the late afternoon when the daughter was still out, the mother had received a telegram, which caused her to settle the bill for the two of them and hurry off in a cab.

"'Are you certain you know whom I'm talking about?' I said to him. 'The woman with the French accent?'

"'Oh, yes,' he said. 'Very high strung. Hard to forget. She has dark features and a bad eye.'"

"That's the one," I said, recalling Stanford's description, "but it sounds as if you never found her."

She held up a hand. "Not done yet, Doctor. Even though the woman had gone, I went up to her rooms anyway and fibbed a bit to get a maid in the hallway to unlock the door. 'My friend forgot something inside before checking out,' I lied, 'and she asked me to look for it.'"

Holmes clapped his hands in appreciation. "What did you discover?"

"Well, the French woman obviously had left most of her things behind. The room was in disarray." Mrs. Rohlfs waved her arms about to dramatize the chaos. "There were two trunks, both open, their contents strewn about. Clothes were tossed onto the bed. An empty notebook was lying on the floor. I'm guessing this Madame Costerd was looking for something; and whether she found it or not, she seems to have gone off in quite a hurry."

"Perhaps, she received word of what had happened to her daughter in the museum," I suggested.

"But how, Watson?" Holmes asked. "From whom? And even if that were the case, it seems more likely that rather than disappearing, she would have gone to the museum as quickly as possible to aid the girl. We must discover what made the lady vanish and where she went."

"If I were writing one of my mysteries about all this," observed Mrs. Rohlfs, "I'd say that maybe this Madame Costerd had something to do with the poor girl's death. Much as I hate to think about it, she did send the girl to the museum on her own."

Having delivered to us that disturbing hypothesis, Mrs. Rohlfs paraded out the door.

"Do enjoy yourself at Hamley's," I shouted after her. Swirling in my brain, however, were grotesque images of a deranged Robin Hood letting fly deadly arrows into innocent maidens. It was with relief that I joined Holmes and his mannequin-friend on the morning's cab ride back to the British Museum.

The cabbie joked that the dummy could ride gratis in our drive to Montague Place. Although the thing remained an awkward travel companion, Holmes provided no inkling of what role it was to play.

Langdon Steeples, dressed casually in linen trousers and white shirt that warm summer's day, awaited us at the door to the North Hall. He appeared more ready for sport than aiding in a murder investigation.

"Ah, Steeples," Holmes said as he extended a hand, "pleased to see you again. Glad my telegram reached you in time."

"Always ready to help, Mr. Holmes," Steeples said, brushing back a tumble of brown hair.

Holmes introduced me to the archer and then moved on to the constable at the door, requesting the policeman inform Lestrade that we had arrived.

The inspector met us just inside the doorway. Flicking his head in the direction of the mannequin, he asked with a straight face, "Who's this then?"

"Assistant to the archer," Holmes answered with an equally impassive mien.

Lestrade looked Steeples up and down. "A bowman, eh? Let's get him going."

Beneath the glare of the electric lighting, the inspector led us up the stairs and turned to the walkway on the right. Whilst Holmes and Steeples followed him to the gallery with the wall-hanging, I now understood it fell upon me to carry the mannequin to the scene of the young girl's death. In the appropriate position, it was to serve as target practice for Steeples. As Holmes had instructed, I stood the thing at the front of the railing in the spot I had chalked the previous day.

On the opposite side, I could see Holmes direct Steeples to the centre of the gallery. The archer stood back far enough so that the police on the ground floor could not see him—just as the patrons in the museum had reported witnessing no one shoot an arrow from the upper level the day before.

Holmes handed Steeples the nicked bow and a quiver of Norman arrows. The archer flexed the bow and pulled back on its string to test the strength. He then hefted a few of the arrows and, after examining their shafts, selected one to his fancy. It remained for him only to look across the stairwell to be certain that I was safely out of the line of fire. From behind a wall, I leaned out and waved that he could proceed.

Careful to expose little of my person, I peered round my protective cover to watch the proceedings. Standing tall and perpendicular to the mannequin, Steeples assumed the classic bowman's pose—feet apart, eyes siting his target along the shaft, the nock of the arrow gently nestling against the bowstring which he pulled back to his cheek. As he raised the bow ever so slightly to allow for distance and trajectory, I leaned back out of range, and Steeples let the arrow fly.

Swiftly it came, hissing over the stairwell; and I watched it slam into the mannequin and bring it down. Though nothing live had been struck, the penetrating thump was sickening none the less. One needed no grand imagination to conjure in that lifeless blow the reality of the cruel bodkin-arrowhead ripping through the flesh of that young innocent and crashing into bone.

I swallowed hard; yet even as I rushed over to examine the so-called wound, I could see that the puncture was too close to the dummy's right side— in short, a failed replication of the actual tear in the centre of the poor girl's chest.

"No!" I shouted to Holmes and watched him move Steeples to a new spot between the right-hand urn and the wall where young Stanford said he had hidden.

I prepared the mannequin once more, and this time Steeples crouched low and shot through the opening between the wall and the inward curve at the base of the urn. Once more the arrow crossed high over the stairs, but on this second attempt it ended up clattering to the tiles a few feet from the dummy.

"No good, Mr. Holmes," I barely heard Steeples say. "From this position I can't get off a clean shot and hit the target."

At the very least, such a conclusion added legitimacy to Stanford's claim of innocence.

For Steeples' third attempt, Sherlock Holmes stationed the archer in the narrow gap between the back-wall and the left-hand pedestal. As in his previous shot, Steeples bent low to enable the arrow to pass through the space between the lower curve of the urn and the top of the pedestal.

"Ready, Watson?" Holmes shouted.

I responded with another wave, leaned back behind my cover, and this time saw the arrow smash directly into the heart of the dummy. I hastened to it and discovered exactly what I had expected—the same cruel cut in the centre of the mannequin's chest that I had witnessed in the breast of the poor human victim. I raised a hand to signal success.

Holmes congratulated Steeples and thanked him for his invaluable work. In a word, with the aid of the Cambridge Bowman, we had discovered the lair of the killer.

Although the police had closed the North Hall the day following the murder, the rest of the British Museum remained open to visitors. Which meant that the various charwomen were on hand as well.

"With all due respect, Mr. Holmes, what you're doing is a waste of your time." Thus, Lestrade responded to Holmes's intention to interview the women whose job it was to clean the museum. "Not a one was actually inside the Hastings exhibit at the time the girl was killed."

"No imagination," Holmes muttered, even as Lestrade instructed a constable to facilitate our passage through the museum's main entrance round the corner in Great Russell Street. Once inside, Holmes and I edged our way through the clusters of tourists come to ogle the antiquities and gawp at the vast domed reading-room.

Though Holmes had utilised the room's rich resources not long before when he had investigated the background of Jack Stapleton in the Baskerville case, on this occasion we were simply making our way through the circular chamber to locate the employees' stairs at the rear of the building. It was in the basement, the Curator had told us, that we would find the room reserved for the workers who actually enabled the museum to function.

The chamber itself was filled with simple wooden tables and chairs and surrounded by narrow closets that held jackets, coats, and other personal items. A dark, bearded fellow in a grey uniform looked to be in charge. Upon being asked to find the charwomen, he ran his finger down a list of names on a chart pinned to a wall.

"Three women sweep the Northern Hall," he said. "Right now, they're on the ground floor—two are somewhere in the Assyrian rooms, t'other, in the Egyptian."

Holmes and I were familiar enough with the collections from the ancient world to locate the cleaners without any difficulty. We found the first two between a pair of Assyrian Lamasi, those huge, human-headed, winged-bull statues that used to guard the entrances to imposing palaces. The greyish-blue limestone figures towered over the women who, despite the divine inspiration surrounding them, had nothing to offer concerning our murder enquiry.

It was not until we interviewed the third cleaner that we were rewarded for our troubles. We found her washing the concrete floor of a little-used corridor in the Egyptian collection. She was working just beyond the pair of red-granite lions said to symbolise the Egyptian king Amenhotep.

"We are investigating the murder of that poor girl in the Hastings exhibit, Madam," Holmes addressed her.

She looked up from where she had settled on her knees to do her work. "The one killed by an arrow yesterday, do you mean?"

"Quite so."

"Terrible," the woman said, shaking her head. "But what's it got to do with me?"

"We believe the arrow was shot with a bow that had a nick—a chip—at the top. At some point it was stored beneath the Curator's office, and we would like to know if you have ever seen such a thing?"

"A bow with a nick in it, you say?" Tossing her scrub brush into the bucket of soapy water, she slowly stood up. "Mebbe I have seen sich a bow—but not in the cellar. In the Curator's closet, I think."

"The Curator's closet, you say?" Holmes repeated. "The one next to his office?"

Niven had noticed the bow in the cellar; if this woman were to be believed, somehow it had made its way up to the ground floor.

"Yeh," she said, her recall sounding more confident now. "Behind some rolled up-rugs it was. The bow fell over when I was sweeping. That's the only reason I seen it. A beat-up thing like that don't belong in the closet. That's why I remember it at all. Pieces like that, the ones with something wrong—they store them down below in the Curator's cellar."

"It had been there originally," Holmes explained. "But obviously someone brought it up to the closet and placed it behind those rugs. You wouldn't by any chance know how it got there—who might have put it there?"

"No. Sorry, luv. Can't rightly say, can I?"

"Well, then, let me ask how long ago it was that you saw it?"

"Mebbe a fortnight. Can't rightly say," she repeated.

Holmes looked my way to see if I had any questions. When I remained silent, he said to the woman, "Thank you very much. You've helped our investigation greatly."

The woman smiled, revealing a missing pair of front teeth. "Don't usually get much appreciation round here." Then she kneeled down and got back to her scrubbing.

"Surely, you can't be suggesting that Mr. Last had something to do with the murder," said Lestrade after Holmes had told him what we had just learned from the charwoman. "He told me he was in another gallery when the arrow flew, and I believe him. Mr. Last—a murderous archer? Pull my other leg."

But Holmes would not be put off. "Keep in mind, Lestrade, that in his youth Mr. Last was quite the athlete. What's more, regardless of wherever the man says he was when the arrow was fired, we must still account for who moved the bow from the cellar to his closet; who transported it from his closet to the spot behind the tapestry; and once there, who strung it. It takes someone familiar with the sport to fix a bowstring properly.

"True, Mr. Holmes, but the Curator—"

"If Niven is to be believed," Holmes went on, "at the time of the murder, Niven himself was the only person in the small staircase at the rear of the hall. Thus, it is most important that we examine the only remaining egress to the ground floor besides the grand staircase. I refer, of course, to the stairs behind the tapestry that lead down to Last's office."

Hearing no objections, Holmes marched off to the door at the foot of the staircase in question, and Lestrade and I followed.

Unfortunately, the Curator himself was home ill. Worse, after learning of the murder, he had pocketed his museum keys, which were now also at his home. Yet Holmes would not be denied. Producing his lock picks, he unlocked the door within seconds and opened it wide.

Darkness blanketed the stairwell beyond. Not even all the startling electric illumination within the hall could reach the set of stairs beyond the doorway.

"Not to worry, Mr. Holmes," cautioned Lestrade as he ordered one of the uniformed constables standing by to procure a lantern from the police van just outside the building.

Moments later, holding before him a dark lantern, whose sliding shutter could focus a beam of light on a particular spot, Sherlock Holmes penetrated the gloom of the stairwell. In fascination, I watched the narrow ray of light as it moved from side to side and then slowly upward, illuminating Holmes's long fingers as, beneath the scrutiny of his magnifying lens, he carefully ran a hand along the surface of each step.

Upon reaching the landing at the top, he turned about and made his way back down. "We have been informed by Niven that this stairway is never used," he announced, "and yet it has been trod quite recently. The disturbed dust reveals the story.

"A man in rubbers made a quick dash up and down these stairs not long ago and then a second run down in regular shoes. I suggest that the trip in rubbers not only disguised a distinctive boot but more importantly muffled the sound of carrying the bow from the Curator's closet to its hiding place behind the tapestry. The trip down in similarly-sized regular shoes no doubt took place after the shooting—an escape through the Curator's office, if you will."

"Why no footmarks from the regular shoe going *up*, Mr. Holmes?" Lestrade asked.

"No need for the archer to have gone up these stairs to shoot the arrow if he began his deadly mission already on the upper floor. After assuring himself that no one was watching, he could have reached behind the tapestry and recovered the bow from where he had secreted it earlier. Unobserved, he could have slipped in behind the left-hand pedestal, strung the bow, and prepared his deadly shot with an arrow he had most likely concealed within his clothing."

"Blimey," said Lestrade, stroking his chin. "You may be right, Mr. Holmes." He stroked his chin one more time and added, "but then again you might also be wrong. All this one-time-up and two-times-down—mere speculation. Concealed arrow? Where's the proof?

"Sorry, Mr. Holmes, but with all due respect, what seems much more likely— 'elementary' I believe you like to call it—is that, just as the attendant Niven has already told us, someone with access to the Curator's office—that is, virtually anyone who works here—used the key on the spur of the moment to open the door, climb up the stairs, step into the gallery, and shoot the arrow into a beautiful young girl. Why, it boils the blood just to think about it."

"And yet," said Holmes, "you cannot dismiss the premeditation to which the hidden bow and a concealed arrow attest. With the Curator's cellar, closet, and recessed stairway so crucial to the murder, one must assume that our killer moves with a degree of ease among the more distinguished members of the museum administrators."

Lestrade raised his eyebrows in disbelief. "Again, Mr. Holmes? You cannot be accusing the Curator or the Director. Why, neither one was in the immediate vicinity of the tragedy. No, sir. They are beyond reproach."

Holmes said nothing, prompting Lestrade to bolster his own view. "Remember that there are other suspects to consider. One of the two doormen went missing from his post at the exact moment of the shooting. To be fair, he explained his movements in terms of the newlywed couple whom he says he stopped from being affectionate in public. We have the names of the man and woman in question, so we will be able to verify his account."

"No doubt they will substantiate his story," I offered. "No one would be foolish enough to invent a tale so easily denied."

A grin crossed the inspector's face. "My thinking exactly, Doctor. The doorman won't do. But the museum attendant, Niven Redmond, will. I intend to charge the villain with the murder of that innocent girl."

"Why, it was Niven who showed us the bow!" I exclaimed. "He's the one who called out the alarm that prompted the doormen to lock the building. Why behave in such a fashion if he is indeed the murderer?"

"I've given that a bit of thought as well," said Lestrade. "Calling out as Niven did removes himself from suspicion. It deflects any criticism thrown his way, sends charges against him in different directions—in a word, puts us on the wrong scent. But we won't allow ourselves to be misled."

When Lestrade developed a theory, he was not one to be dissuaded. He stood tall as he proclaimed, "Niven Redmond knew of the bow in the cellar; he knew of the stairs behind the tapestry; he knew of the key to the stairway. He appears as capable as anyone of performing the hellish deed."

"Anything else?" Holmes asked sceptically.

"As a matter of fact, Mr. Holmes, there is. Scotland Yard did some investigating and turned up some interesting facts about Niven Redmond. Not only does he plan to marry soon, but he's also been very active in sport—rugby, football, and—listen carefully, gentlemen—archery. What's more, he's said to be a bit of a gambler. Dare I say I am nothing if not practical. Only after I view the evidence do I draw my conclusion. This Niven Redmond is our man."

Though Holmes and I both knew that Niven's jacket had revealed no clues, Holmes allowed the inspector to continue his fantasy. "If you are correct, Lestrade," said my friend, "what could have prompted Niven to kill this poor girl?"

"Can't be sure, of course, Mr. Holmes—but the man is about to be married. Maybe he needed money. Perhaps someone challenged him with a dare: Hit a target they'd agreed upon in the Hastings exhibit—a hauberk, perhaps, or a helmet—and win some cash. Maybe he took the shot, and the girl got in the way. Who knows? Sooner or later, we'll get it out of him. Not to worry. I'm leaving right now to make the arrest."

Holmes shrugged as we watched Lestrade stride hurriedly toward the museum's exit. "Come, Watson," he said once the door had shut. "Let us return to Baker Street. Perhaps we can make more sense of this matter than the inspector has."

Part II

On the Trail

3 June 1890 — 7 June 1890

Chapter Seven

Developments

The motive behind nine-tenths
of the crime in the world
is selfishness.
>--Anna Katharine Green
>"Why Human Beings are
>Interested in Crime"
>*American Magazine*,
>February 1919

Sipping tea later that afternoon, Sherlock Holmes looked up from the sheet of paper on the table before him. "I know Lestrade," he said laying down his pen. "He is far too content with the man he is arresting to be concerned with other threads of the case."

"Which other threads do you have in mind?" I wanted to know.

Holmes sipped his tea again, then said, "Take, for instance, Madame Costerd, the victim's mother. Does it not seem strange to you that upon receiving a telegram at the time her daughter was off at the British Museum, she would drop everything, check the two of them out of the hotel, and then quickly disappear into the void of this great metropolis?"

"Of course, it seems strange," I replied, "and yet she appears to have been nowhere near the museum when Angelique was killed. Lestrade would argue that she has no bearing on the murder itself."

"Lestrade could so argue, but I will not. There is most definitely a connection, and I intend to discover what it is. Thus, we must find this Madame Costerd. To that end"—here he handed me what he had been writing— "I plan to have this notice appear in the morning prints":

> *A reward will be given to anyone providing information regarding Mme. Marie Costerd, a French woman who arrived from Calais on second June with her daughter, Angelique. She registered at Brown's Hotel, but left in a rush later that afternoon, and she has not been heard from since. She may be distinguished by her dark complexion and drooping left eyelid. Reply: 221B Baker Street.*

"Let us hope for a quick response," I said.

Early the next morning, we heard light footfalls on the stairs and thought they might be heralding a swift reaction to Holmes's advert. As it turned out, however, the soft tread belonged to Mrs. Rohlfs.

"I just reclaimed my hat," she announced, pointing with the hand that held her reticule to the wide-brimmed, straw-hat atop her head. Artificial red poppies were attached to the front of the crown. "It's the one I left on a cloakroom hook at the museum on Monday."

What the other hand was holding, however, interested us more—a folded grey coat very much resembling the morning attire described by Mrs. Rohlfs that had been worn by the Curator and the Director on the day of the murder.

Mrs. Rohlfs followed our gaze. "I know you're interested in the coats the men had on," she said. "So, naturally, an old beggar wearing this one would attract my attention. I saw him just as I was leaving the museum with my hat—a skinny old fellow, standing in front of a corner pub."

"The Alpha Inn," I said, a small but not unfamiliar stop for Holmes and me across the road from the British Museum. (Readers may remember the Alpha as the meeting place of the so-called "goose-club," which I described in connection with the curious theft of the Blue Carbuncle.)

"The coat caught my eye," Mrs. Rohlfs went on, "because compared to the rest of his shabby clothing, it looked altogether too smart, if you take my meaning."

Holmes leaned forward, obviously sensing where Mrs. Rohlfs was leading.

"In fact, at the risk of putting too fine a point on it, gentlemen, the coat looked very much like the grey cutaways the Curator and the Director were wearing on Monday. Once I approached the poor fellow, I could even see the holes in the lapel made by the museum pin."

"Most perceptive, Mrs. Rohlfs," Holmes nodded.

The American lady beamed at Holmes's encouragement. "'If you don't mind my asking,' I said to the old man, 'where did you get that coat?'

"He offered a toothless smile while he ran his wrinkled hands up and down the lapels as if to show off his finery." Mrs. Rohlfs mimed the action as she described it. "'Got it early this morning from the Salvation Army ladies over there,' he said with a flick of his head.

"I turned to see a pair of bonneted women across the street in front of the museum. They were wearing navy-blue dresses with double rows of buttons and standing by the kerb behind a table filled with a collection of shirts and coats and trousers. I was close enough to make out the silver S's on their collars as they handed out clothing to the needy.

"Now that he had an audience, the old man was more than willing to talk. 'Some toff in the museum was giving things away, the lady said. The coat was too big for 'im, she said. I say, 'is misfortune; my good luck. All I know is, it fits me fine.' And he stroked the lapels again."

"Good luck indeed," I observed. "The old man had reason to be pleased."

"To be sure," said Mrs. Rohlfs, "except that suddenly he changed his attitude. He wrapped his arms around himself, took a step backward, and said, "'ere now, you're not fixing to take this coat away from me.'

"'Oh, no,' I smiled warmly. 'In fact,' I said without thinking much about it, 'I'll buy it from you.' I opened my purse and pulled out some coins. 'Take what's fair,' I told him, and he did just that—I couldn't even tell you how much. Holding the money in his fist, he extricated his arms from the sleeves, gave me the coat, and hobbled off with his new-found wealth. Thin as he was, he looked like he could use some food, but I suspect he will spend the money more recklessly."

I shook my head in disbelief. "You could have been taken unfair advantage of."

"My thought exactly, Doctor," she blushed, "but it was evidence I was procuring. In any case"—at this point, she handed the coat to Holmes— "I thought you'd like to have it."

My friend eagerly took the coat from her and, as he had done with Niven's jacket, held it up and studied it top to bottom and along the sleeves. Finally, he opened it wide and searched the grey interior lining.

"Nothing inside," he announced. "For that matter, nothing outside—if you discount the blood spots at the cuff."

Mrs. Rohlfs and I both started at that bit of news though it did not seem to concern Sherlock Holmes.

He laid the coat over the rail of a chair and turned back to our visitor. "I appreciate both your enthusiasm and your sharp eye, Mrs. Rohlfs," he said. "If you are available, I am certain I will be able to put your talents to future use."

"Thank you, Mr. Holmes," the American lady beamed, "but now I really must be off. Nelly is watching the children, and I have to get back to them." With her hand atop her newly recovered hat, she rushed out the door, down the stairs, and out into Baker Street.

Not an hour after the departure of Mrs. Rohlfs, a second woman came to our door. Of dowdy appearance and at the far end of middle age, she was announced by our page as "Mrs. Amanda Jones." Holmes and I both rose to meet her. In her hand was a newspaper folded back to reveal Holmes's posting.

"You're paying for information?" was the first thing she said.

"If it's worthwhile," Holmes answered.

"Oh, it is, luv," she said, "you can be sure of that. I keep a boarding house for respectable ladies near Paddington Station, and I believe I've seen the woman you was asking about." She raised the newspaper for emphasis. "Don't know nothing about her name— Custard, you say? Called herself Mrs. Smith to me, she did. Mrs. Smith! —and her with a French accent, I should say. But she fits your description all right—dark skin, bad eye. She stayed in one of my rooms the past two nights—Monday and Tuesday, that is."

"And tonight?" I asked.

Mrs. Jones shook her head. "Sorry, luv. She left early this morning without a word. Took her things and was gone. Odd sort, if you ask me."

"In what sense?" Holmes wanted to know.

"You're paying, yeh?" Mrs. Jones repeated. "Like you said here." She waved the newspaper to emphasise her point.

Holmes nodded.

"Well then, in those two days she never went out. Very nervous type. Asked another boarder to bring in all the public prints she could find, didn't she? Oh, the lady paid for them, but she just stayed put. And that wasn't the strangest part. Once she left, I went in to clean, and I found this in the dustbin."

Mrs. Jones withdrew from her purse a small, sepia-coloured photograph—or rather the remnants of one—perhaps five inches square. It had clearly begun as the portrait of a man—bits of collar and lapel were still visible near the bottom—but a small ring of half-inch, circular holes towards the centre had completely destroyed any semblance of a discernible image.

Holmes extended his hand, and Mrs. Jones placed the photograph in it. With his glass, he scrutinised what remained of both sides of the picture and then offered it to me. "Note the printing on the back," he said.

Although the image itself had been destroyed, upon turning over the photograph I could discern a fragment of text in the lower-right corner:

ussell
yck Studio
per Street
ington

"Surely," I said to Holmes, "it's the partial name of the photography studio that produced the portrait. The missing letters are a casualty of whatever created the holes, but the location of the studio itself shouldn't be difficult to find." I looked more closely. "I daresay the last word may be Paddington."

"Excellent, Watson."

"Paddington, is it now?" said Mrs. Jones. "As I told you, my boarding house is near the station."

Holmes ignored her comment. Instead, he asked me, "What do you think caused the damage?"

I turned the photograph over again and looked at the round holes that had eliminated any recognizable representation. As a military doctor, I had seen my share of such perforations. "I should judge they were made by bullets."

"Undoubtedly, old fellow. Five of them to be precise. Most probably from a forty-five-calibre pistol."

"A pistol, you say," cried out Mrs. Jones. "That must be it. A few times during the last two evenings, when a train rumbled past, I swear I heard sharp knocks or cracks coming from Mrs. Smith's room. A pistol would be just the thing. I never thought of a gun, but that would explain it. Never saw no bullets neither—though I did find a pillow on the bed that had its insides torn out. She left some coins on the quilt to level our account."

"I imagine," said Holmes, pointing at the decimated picture in my hand, "that she placed this photograph against the pillow and waited for the roar of the train to mask the sound of gunfire."

"That's one angry witch," observed Mrs. Jones, "though I must say it was decent of her to leave me the extra money. Speaking of which," she said, holding out her hand to Holmes, "if I may be so bold, sir, this photograph, such as it is, and all the information I've given you must be worth an additional sum above the reward you offered. I've come here in good faith, as you can tell."

"Indeed, Mrs. Jones, you've been most helpful." My friend reached into his pocket and produced a pound note, which he handed to the woman.

Raising her eyebrows in appreciation, she beamed, "Thank you very much indeed, sir," and left us.

"Three questions, Watson," Holmes said as soon as he had closed the door. "Whose portrait? What angered Madame Costerd so much that she shot the image to shreds? And, of course, where has the mysterious French woman now taken herself?"

By the time I came down for breakfast Thursday morning, Holmes was already gone. I assumed that our meeting with Mrs. Jones had prompted his early departure, but he had not bothered to share his plans with me.

I was just finishing my coffee when he returned.

"Islington," he responded to my enquiring look. "More precisely, No. 238 Upper Street. The photography shop of one Edward Russell. He calls the place Van Dyke Studio."*

"Islington," I repeated, "not Paddington."

"Sorry, old fellow. I left our mutilated portrait with Mr. Russell. He keeps his original glass-plate negatives; and assuming he finds the one in question, he promised to print a new copy of the photograph for me. Then I was off again, this time to Somerset House. North wing."

I knew the place, of course—the white, Neoclassical structure on the south side of the Strand. The north wing housed the government's registry office.

"I was looking for local marriage certificates," Holmes said. "Costerd is not a common name. With a bit of luck, I thought I might be able to find the record of a relative here in London with

---

*Though Edward John Russell (1830-1895) identified himself as a London photographer as early as 1861, his Van Dyck Studio does not appear in the trade journals until 1894. Since official listings of Russell's occupation appear incomplete, however, Holmes's visit to Russell's studio in 1890 does not seem wildly anachronistic considering the inconsistency of the historical record.

the same surname who might have some thoughts on where to find the elusive woman."

"And?"

"There is an Emil Costerd with an address in St. John's Wood. He was married three years ago, and one can hope that he and his wife still live there."

"Shall we pay them a visit?"

"Actually, I hope to impose upon Mrs. Rohlfs to do the honours. She established an excellent rapport with Mrs. Sommers at the museum and displayed keen insight regarding the beggar and his coat. I believe she will be equally effective with Mrs. Costerd."

"Good thinking, Holmes. I suspect that a couple of gentlemen enquiring about a solitary woman might raise some eyebrows."

"My thinking exactly. If we assume that the husband will be at work during the day, Mrs. Rohlfs should have the wife to herself."

"Woman to woman you mean."

"Quite so," Holmes said, and after writing a brief invitation to the American lady, he called upon Billy the page to convey the request to Brown's.

"I have other plans for the two of us," Holmes said once the lad was gone. "We shall go to the Medallion to see how Mrs. Sommers is getting along. If she is still unwell, presenting a medical man like yourself might be just the ticket for assuring us entry."

At the front-desk of the timber-faced hotel in High Holborn, we enquired after Mrs. Sommers.

"Fainted not a minute after entering the building Monday night," the portly clerk at the desk told us. Though he gave us her room number, he added, "Our house doctor's been attending her ever since."

Holmes pulled me aside. "Go up there in your medical capacity, Watson. See what you can learn and somehow arrange to be notified when she is able to speak to us."

"On my way," I told Holmes and mounted the stairs.

A young nurse in blue dress and white apron answered my knock on Mrs. Sommers' door. I told the nurse my business, and she presented me to the hotel doctor, a tall, older man with a pointed white beard. He wore a pince-nez and seemed to enjoy looking down at people through its lenses.

"No need for anyone else to see the patient," he proclaimed, positioning himself directly in front of the door to Mrs. Sommers' bedroom. I had met such professionals before, the kind who seem more interested in preventing another doctor from moving in on their patients than worrying about the patients' well-being. There would be no getting round his territorial defence.

On the other hand, I was not about to be denied. Thanks to her sharp eyes and commiserating smile, I sensed in the nurse a sensitive professional who understood the impediment I was confronting. Even as the doctor was showing me out, I surreptitiously motioned her to step into the hotel corridor.

"I am Dr. John Watson," I told her a few moments later when she was able to join me. "My associate and I are investigating the murder of that poor girl in the museum that your patient was witness to, and—"

"It was just awful," she said, "a young girl like that struck down by an arrow. I'll do anything I can to help."

"We most urgently need to speak with your patient. Has she said anything at all?"

The nurse offered a crooked smile. "A bit strange, don't you know? On occasion, she's murmured something about that ship, the famous one with the mutiny."

"The *Bounty*?" I asked.

"Aye, that's the one. She's called it out a few times and the sea as well. I didn't know what to make of it."

Nor did I. Some sort of mental fog, I feared. Lestrade had called it "madness", and perhaps he was correct. In any case, I wrote Holmes's address on the back of one of my business cards and handed it to her. "When Mrs. Sommers is able to speak, please contact us at this address. I imagine that her current doctor has no interest in uncovering the shock that has so disabled her."

The nurse gave me a smile of confirmation and slipped the card into her apron pocket. "Whatever I can do to help," she repeated softly and retreated through the doorway where once more she fell under the critical eye of the doctor.

"Well done, old chap," Holmes congratulated me when I reported back to him downstairs. "Now we must return to Baker Street and see if our American friend has agreed to question Mrs. Costerd tomorrow. I can't imagine that she will turn down the opportunity to participate in the kind of investigation that until now she has only written about in her fiction."

Chapter Eight

Mrs. Rohlfs's Account

Why, sometimes I have had people come to me
with half-formed ideas of some remarkable thing
that has happened in life, and I have had to moderate it in
order to make it sound plausible.
> --Anna Katharine Green
> Quoted by Ruth Snyder,
> "Life's Facts as Startling as
> Fiction, Says Writer, 76"
> *Indianapolis Sunday Star*
> May 13, 1928

*W*ith apologies to Jane Austen (another female novelist of some renown), I believe it is also a truth universally acknowledged that a crime writer in search of a plot will strive to seek out a story with the dogged determination of the most indefatigable detective. How else to explain Mrs. Rohlfs's eagerness that Friday morning to help Sherlock Holmes solve the murder at the British Museum?

Having quickly agreed to Holmes's request the day before, she arrived at 221B not long after breakfast. On this occasion, she was dressed in a long-sleeved, high-necked dress of light-blue cotton with white trim, white gloves, and a navy-blue sash tied at the waist.

"Are you joking, Mr. Holmes?" the voluble Mrs. Rohlfs exclaimed when my friend asked if she was certain she wanted to aid his enquiry. "I seek inspiration from all available sources—in point of fact, true stories are my foundation."

"Grist for the novelist's mill," I observed.

"Grist, indeed, Doctor. Not only do I rely on newspaper accounts of the most wicked murders, but also on the clippings and articles about such crimes that friends and relatives constantly send me. With a twist here and an exaggeration there, I convert those realities into my own fictions."

"Quite different from my own process," I felt compelled to say. "I simply note the events as they happen."

To my great relief, Sherlock Holmes, forever complaining about what he calls my tendency to embellish, said nothing.

"My late father in particular," Mrs. Rohlfs continued, "offered me many ideas. He was a criminal attorney in New York with loads of connections to local government. Who knows? I don't wish to sound callous—after all, a poor innocent was horribly killed in the museum this past Monday—but perhaps something positive can arise from my own involvement in the tragedy. What would you have me do?"

"I would like you to interview Mrs. Emil Costerd, the presumed sister-in-law of Marie Costerd, mother of the poor girl killed in the North Hall. In point of fact, you already have a faint connection to the French woman. Not only did you discover her name at Brown's, but you also searched her rooms there."

"That's true," agreed Mrs. Rohlfs.

"I have found what I expect is the sister-in-law's address," said Holmes. "Assuming her husband will be at work, I believe that a persistent questioner like yourself will be able to elicit more information from the woman than Dr. Watson or I ever could."

"Persistent, eh?" Mrs. Rohlfs blushed. "I'll take that as a compliment. What's more, my father would be proud to have heard you say that, for I learned interviewing techniques at his knee. In fact, I've based many of Detective Gryce's low-key interrogations on my father's approach."

"Do you have the time for such an assignment?" I asked. "I worry about your family."

"You may ease your mind, Doctor. Nelly's taking the children to the Royal Zoo today, and Charles is visiting a foundry. So, yes, I am pleased to accept your invitation to take a crack at the interview."

"Excellent," Holmes said. "I envision our current investigation involving the three of us. You, Mrs. Rohlfs, will interview Madame Costerd; you, Watson, shall go see the Curator and verify his reason for giving away his clothing. And I shall pay a visit to the home of Director Aynesworth, another possible owner of a notable coat."

I escorted Mrs. Rohlfs downstairs and out onto the sidewalk. Just then the sun was shining brightly, but I reckoned that the grey clouds off in the distance would be upon us within the hour. Hopefully, rain would not interfere with our plans.

I signalled for a cab and upon its arrival gave the driver the Costerds' address in St. John's Wood.

Moments later, the hansom joined the stream of carriages filling up Baker Street.

I expected to find Holmes in the sitting room upon my return, but the room was empty. I did hear him puttering about in his bedroom, however; and not long thereafter, he emerged on the stairs sporting a long, grizzled beard; a knit cap; a large, baggy coat; a workman's rough trousers; and a pair of scuffed boots. Clearly, Holmes had some plan in mind that only he understood.

It was under threatening skies that Sherlock Holmes and I parted for our different destinations— he (in his workman's disguise) to Director Aynesworth's house in Eaton Square; I (in my normal attire) to Curator Last's office in the British Museum.

I was hoping access to Anthony Last would be as easy as my thirty-minute walk to Bloomsbury, but I found his officious, gap-toothed clerk unwilling to offer me admission. "No appointment?" he queried, flashing a disingenuous smile. "Sorry, Mr. Last is otherwise engaged."

I handed the man my card. "Please, give this to the Curator and tell him that I should like to talk with him regarding the murder of that poor girl in his museum."

The man returned a moment later. "Mr. Last is speaking only to police. Sorry," he said again with the same condescending smirk.

By now I was angry. The Curator had been absent the day we examined the suspicious staircase connected to his office, and now he appeared uninterested in talking to me. "Tell Mr. Last that I have questions regarding the coat he was wearing on Monday—the coat," I added cryptically, "that we know he has since given away."

At this last bit of news, the clerk's pomposity seemed to deflate. In a matter of minutes, I was invited into the Curator's office where Anthony Last was sitting at his massive mahogany desk. On one end of its mirror-like surface stood a copper-coloured antique globe; on the other, a Grecian urn in browns and blacks. Last gestured towards the leather chair facing him.

Though it was I who had come to question *him*, no sooner did I sit down than he posed his own pointed queries. "What's this about my coat? You're not suggesting anything sinister, are you?"

"Two days after the murder, Mr. Last, the coat you wore the day the poor girl was killed was discovered upon the back of a vagrant not far from the museum."

"Very possible," he said. "I cleaned out my belongings, you see. Didn't like the idea that the infernal bow that caused all this grief could be hidden in my own closet behind a collection of jackets and coats most of which I don't even wear. They were a trifle large, don't you know?"

I did not know, but I reckoned a man as thin as Anthony Last would have little trouble squeezing into the narrow space from which the arrow had been loosed.

The Curator continued his explanation. "I had an attendant give a few of my coats and a box of old books to the women helping the poor just outside our door."

"And the blood upon the cuff?" I asked.

Mr. Last frowned. "Didn't know about that. Probably picked it up when I went to the poor girl's side and tried to help the unhappy lady who was kneeling over her—Mrs. Sommers, wasn't it? Another woman was also there, and the two of us tried to get the lady to her feet."

The other woman was, of course. Mrs. Rohlfs, but apparently Mr. Last had not bothered to get her name.

"That's really all I know about the horrible affair. A girl like that, shot dead in my museum. . . . I cannot imagine how such a terrible thing could happen in so august a place as this." He held out his arms to dramatize the breadth of the museum's reach. Beyond the expansive gesture, he had nothing more to add and simply shook his head.

I thanked the Curator for his help and stood up. His explanation had sounded reasonable enough, yet he was still shaking his head as I left the office.

Later that afternoon, Mrs. Rohlfs returned to 221B. Since Holmes had not yet come back, it was up to me to hear whatever revelatory information she might have gathered concerning Marie Costerd. Hopefully, it would be more helpful than the little I had gleaned from the Curator.

At this point, I need not repeat that Mrs. Rohlfs is an excellent story-teller. Yet I caution the critical reader not to be put off if her account seems less the words of a simple visitor to the Costerd house than the iterations of a literary narrator—or, as one might reasonably expect from Anna Katharine Green in particular, the book-like descriptions of a professional novelist. The woman possessed quite the eye for accuracy, and I for one eagerly anticipated what she was going to say.

Perched at the edge of the chair opposite me, she began with her arrival: "The hansom stopped before a small, yellow-gabled house in St. John's Wood. Mr. Holmes had gotten it right—Emil Costerd was not at home. I learned later that he's an attorney and was at work in chambers in Lincoln's Inn Fields."

"It was Mrs. Costerd herself who opened the door. She wore her blonde hair under a green scarf and was dressed in a faded shirtwaist and dark skirt. She greeted me with a sleeping infant on her hip and a questioning smile on her lips. I nodded at the sight of the baby and told her I have two of my own. She responded with the same questioning smile.

"I approached Mrs. Costerd with directness," Mrs. Rohlfs reported. "I told her, 'I have reason to believe that you are related to Madame Marie

Costerd, a French woman whom my associates and I are looking for.'

"The smile immediately faded. 'Who are you?' she wanted to know.

"I gave her my name and told her I was working with a private detective regarding the police investigation into the horrific death of that poor girl at the British Museum on Monday.

"Mrs. Costerd gasped at the reference. 'Surely, you're not suggesting that Marie had some connection to that terrible event.'

"I shook my head. 'No,' I reassured her. 'We know that she was nowhere near the museum on Monday. But I'm afraid she may have some knowledge concerning a person involved.'"

"Nicely done," I complimented Mrs. Rohlfs.

"Thanks, Doctor, but Mrs. Costerd remained doubtful. None the less, with a sigh of resignation and a gentle bounce of the baby, she invited me in and offered me a chair in the sitting room.

"Still holding the baby, she carefully eased herself down onto the couch across from me. 'I speak to you,' she said, 'only because my husband—he's a barrister, you see—told me to be honest in answering any questions involving his sister. He's lived in England for many years whilst his sister—that is, Marie—has remained in France.

"'With her daughter,' I added, but all Mrs. Costerd said was, 'I can't imagine how you knew to seek her here.' She paused a moment, as if to gain courage, then said, 'Yes, Marie did come stay with us. She wrote last week to inform us of her plan. In fact, she got here this past Wednesday afternoon terribly upset and left early yesterday morning. Both Emil and I were quite worried about her—frantic as she was—but before you ask, we have no idea where she went.'

"'Did she tell you what was bothering her?" I questioned.

"'No,' came the short answer. 'It was obvious that Marie was distressed; yet she told us nothing about what had so disturbed her. All she said was that she needed a place to stay for the night and then she would be on her way. She was travelling light, she told me upon her arrival, and required time that afternoon to make some purchases. Really, that's all I know.' With those words, Mrs. Costerd stopped talking and began dandling the baby who was beginning to wake up."

At what I thought was the end of Mrs. Rohlfs's report, I clasped my hands together in a sign of appreciation. "Amazing that you got that much from her. Thank you very much indeed."

Mrs. Rohlfs raised a white-gloved hand to fend me off. "Not done yet, Doctor," she said as she had replied to me once before when I had underestimated her success. "As I was thanking Mrs. Costerd for her help, you see, I was already contemplating the purchases a French woman 'travelling light' would have to make in order to facilitate her get-away. Since vacating the hotel on Monday, she basically had been on the move; and she appeared to have taken next to nothing with her. As a woman myself, I knew she must have needed to purchase something or other to enable her to keep travelling."

"Good thinking," I said. "What happened next?"

"No sooner did I leave the Costerd house than I noticed two shops across the street—one, a chemist; the other, a dressmaker—both promising stops for a woman in need of necessities for travel. Perhaps, Madame Costerd had visited them before leaving. I knew that my Inspector Gryce would want to find out; I know I did.

"'Yes, indeed,' the chemist, a balding man in a long grey apron, told me. 'A French woman came in yesterday afternoon. She bought tooth powder, soap, and other items a lady might require on a trip.'

"'Did she mention where she was going?' I asked.

"The chemist shook his head. 'No, she made her purchases, put them in a Gladstone, and left. However, I do believe she stopped in at the shop next door—ladies' furnishings.' He nodded in the direction of his neighbour. 'You could enquire there.'

"I tried a different approach with the dressmaker, a middle-aged woman in a fashionable suit of green silk. 'My friend Marie, a French woman, came in here yesterday.'

"'Oh, yes,' the woman remembered, 'she purchased a number of fabrics, which she planned to have fashioned into skirts. The collection was too much for her to carry, so she paid for me to ship it.'

"I struggled to contain my excitement—this shopkeeper must know Madame Costerd's next destination. 'Well,' I improvised, 'Marie asked me to send her an additional piece. She had forgotten to select something in—' I searched for a colour that I could assume the conservative Madame Costerd would not have selected— 'in yellow.'"

"Well done," I said.

"I can assure you that the shopkeeper was surprised. "'Yellow!' she exclaimed. 'Quite different from the browns and greys she chose on her own.'

"I shrugged and ordered three yards of yellow worsted. As the woman was cutting it, I told her that I would ship the fabric myself and, holding my breath, asked for the address Marie had given.

"'Not your concern,' the woman replied. 'I've already included the shipping fee in your order, so the transit will be taken care of. In fact, the postman will be making his rounds within the hour, and I can have your order ready for him to pick up by then.'

"I don't need to tell you, Doctor, that I felt stymied. The shopkeeper had the information we wanted, and yet I couldn't argue with the lady without raising some sort of suspicion. I had just sixty minutes to think up a plan before the postman arrived."

"And what did you decide to do?"

"Lucky for me, I didn't have to wait the full hour to implement my strategy. About thirty minutes later, I watched from around the corner as the postman in his grey suit and little round cap approached the dressmaker's shop. A few minutes later, he emerged carrying the large, brown-paper package containing what I assumed was the fabric I had purchased for Madame Costerd.

"I was ready. I approached the unsuspecting postman from the opposite direction. As I walked towards the poor fellow, I pretended to fumble inside my purse as if I were looking for something. With my head down, I managed to bump full force into the man. As I had intended, the collision sent the package flying."

"Good show!" I exclaimed.

"'So sorry,' the postman said though it was completely my fault. Despite stumbling about, he made a move to retrieve the package.

"But I was faster. I snatched it up and ambled slowly towards him. In the process, I was just able to read the destination on the shipping label—which, of course, had been my intent all along."

"Good show," I repeated. "Where is she staying?"

"I suppose you've asked the correct question, Doctor; but, you see, strangely, the package was not addressed to Marie Costerd at all. Instead, it was being sent to someone named Emmeline Ford at a house called 'The Spinney' in Kendal—though I have no idea where such a place even is."

"Kendal's a market town to the north in the lower part of the Lake District. It's been a trading centre for centuries."

"I was right. I figured you or Mr. Holmes would know. But at that moment, it didn't really matter; I had no time for thinking about unknown locations. I had to return the package to the poor postman. So as sweetly as I could, I said, 'I beg your pardon,' and handed the parcel back to the man.

"He touched the bill of his cap and thanked me most appreciatively yet again—as if *he* had been responsible for the entire incident. Once he'd moved on, I found a cab and made my way back here to Baker Street."

I could only shake my head in wonder. With such talent, the woman could put to shame the detectives of the Metropolitan Police. At the very least, I could envision such skills appearing in some fictional female detective in Mrs. Rohlfs's literary future.[*]

"I assume that you and Mr. Holmes will go to Kendal," said Mrs. Rohlfs. "I for one cannot continue leaving my children in the hands of their nurse or their father for so long. Children do need their mother, you know."

"Of course, of course," I said. "Couldn't agree more, Mrs. Rohlfs. In any case, it's too late to do anything today. Rest assured, however, that we will go to Kendal and investigate this further. Of that I am certain."

I escorted Mrs. Rohlfs down to the street.

"The weather is changing," she noted. "Not at all like our warm summers in Buffalo."

---

[*] Dr. Watson's prediction was quite accurate with Anna Katharine Green's later invention of two female sleuths, Miss Amelia Butterworth (said to be an influence on Agatha Christie's Miss Marple) and Violet Strange, private investigator for the upper classes. Contemporary mystery writer Sara Paretsky has written a Sherlock Holmes pastiche, "The Curious Affair of the Italian Art Dealer," which pays homage to Mrs. Butterworth as well as to Detective Gryce.

A chill was indeed in the air; what had begun as a bright, sunny day continued to darken. Beneath the gloomy rain-clouds then scudding across the sky, I flagged a hansom to convey Mrs. Rohlfs to her hotel.

During my climb back up the stairs, I realised that I had no idea when Sherlock Holmes was going to return. In point of fact, I expected him later that evening; but in the off-chance that he did not come home by then—let alone by morning—I reckoned it would fall upon me—rain or no rain—to prevent the trail of the missing Madame Costerd from growing cold.

Chapter Nine

The Lake District

I should not advise people to enter upon a literary life
who were not driven to it by all the forces of their being.
--Anna Katharine Green
Quoted by Mary R.P. Hatch
"An American Gaboriau"
The Darby Inter Ocean
Chicago, July 21, 1889

Sherlock Holmes failed to return Friday night, and Mrs. Rohlfs sought time with her family during the weekend. It became my responsibility, therefore, to act upon her report and attempt to track down the elusive Marie Costerd in Kendal.

A few patches of bright sky shone in the distance Saturday morning though the grey clouds I had seen the night before still hovered above the city. At the very least, a brief rain seemed imminent. Undaunted, I waved my furled umbrella and secured a cab for the drive to Euston Station. It was there that I boarded the north-bound train for Lancaster, the junction for the branch line to Kendal.

Despite the early hour and the possible rain that summer's day, I expected to see more travellers on board, more walking sticks, more rucksacks. With an increasing number of trains heading to the Lake

District in recent years, the cost of railway tickets had dropped; and as a result, the carriages were generally filled with day-trippers.

It had not always been thus. For decades, plans for a railway that would open the scenic Lake District to tourists had been opposed by traditional lovers of nature. Almost fifty years earlier, Wordsworth had complained: "Is then no nook of English ground secure from rash assault?"

The shriek of the whistle interrupted my ruminations though the train's slow acceleration past countless grey rooftops and smoking red chimneys provided plenty of time to consider Wordsworth's complaint.

Like the celebrated poet, I too condemn the irreverent among the exalted city-dwellers who seek to turn the nation's treasured landscapes into their personal playgrounds. Indeed, I stand with Mr. Ruskin, who more recently has labelled the intention of the *nouveau riche* to build their oversized vacation homes in the midst of the region's lakes and mountains "a frenzy of avarice".

And yet was not our glorious English countryside a landscape deserving of appreciation by all men? I know that my wife and I certainly thought so. With the branch line from Lancaster now extending past Kendal, it was a simple matter to envision Mary and me beneath the majesty of the Lakeland Fells gazing into the sparkling waters of Lake Windermere.

Still, here was I travelling north on my own to help resolve the museum murder whilst Mary regained her strength some three hundred miles to the south in the heather and woods of the New Forest. This day's trip to Kendal, I vowed, would serve as a forerunner of the vacation she and I would someday enjoy in the Lake District together. I could not know it at the time, of course, but it was an adventure that we were never destined to share.

It goes without saying that I also missed Holmes. Not the most garrulous of railway companions—during how many cases like this one had he sat silently pondering a situation whilst I stared out at the passing countryside? —he nonetheless offered the stability of directing whatever criminal investigation we were pursuing.

Not on this occasion, however. I had to confront on my own the great questions concerning the murder in the North Hall—most problematic of which being who in his right mind could end the life of so innocent a young girl with so fierce a weapon in so dignified a location as the British Museum? Then there was Madame Costerd's connection to the horrible crime, the point of my current railway journey. Why had she fled her hotel, but avoided the scene where her daughter had died, and why was she still on the run?

Ignoring such questions for the time being, I dozed a bit, then scanned the pages of a copy of the *Standard*, which some fellow-traveller had left on a nearby seat. An article about plans for the opening of the Baseball Ground, a pitch for playing the American game in Derby, caught my eye—as if such a game could ever replace cricket to which baseball is often compared. I nodded off again and discovered upon awakening that rain had finally begun to fall, a thin sheet of showers hiding much of the view beyond my window.

At last, however, the massive stone-structured Gate House and the crenelated walls of Lancaster Castle's four towers came into view, and I knew that we would soon be coming to a halt beneath the sandstone steeple of Lancaster Castle Station, where I would be changing trains for further transport north.

Rain followed the railway from Lancaster to the tiny grey-stone station at Kendal. Though the platform was covered, upon leaving the station I immediately found myself in a considerable shower. Pleased that I had brought my brolly, I ventured out into the fierce rain.

Owing to the small number of passengers, I managed to secure a hansom cab, which stood in a covered area to the left of the station. Holding the umbrella high, I reached the carriage without being thoroughly drenched. Beneath a scuffed bowler, a woollen scarf, and a kind of rubberised black cape, the poor driver in anticipation of his next fare sat exposed above and behind the closed carriage he commandeered. No doubt the result of a recent outing, the bowler and cape were beaded with raindrops.

I climbed into the hansom and hoping I sounded surer of myself than I felt, shouted to the driver through the trap door in the ceiling, "The Spinney!" To my surprise, not only did he know the place but its owner, Emmeline Ford, as well.

"Looking to buy?" he shouted back.

"Sorry?"

"Don't you know? Why, Miss Ford, she died last week. The house is going to be sold. Naturally, a gentleman like yourself—I figured you were going to put in a bid. Why else would you be going there? The woman is dead."

"Well, my good man," I replied loudly, "you figured incorrectly. Not interested." But, of course, I was very interested indeed—not in the house, but in the recently departed Miss Ford. Presumably, Madame Costerd did not know that the woman was dead. Else, why would she have sent the cloth to her—let alone made the journey?

And yet there was also the possibility that she had already heard the news and not bothered to make the journey at all. In which case, Mrs. Rohlfs's achievement in securing the Kendal address might simply have provoked me into conducting the proverbial wild-goose chase.

Be that as it may, since here I was and the house itself might offer some answers, I shouted up through the trap door, "Can we get started?"

Edging out into the rain, the cab was soon driving through open countryside. Accompanied by the thrum of water on the roof of the carriage, we drove on; and after a quarter of an hour the driver pulled to a stop in a narrow, muddy road near a group of fir trees—no doubt, the copse responsible for the house's name.

Indeed, not twenty feet before us stood a desolate stone cottage with its shades drawn. Above the black outer door hung a small, wooden plaque, and despite the continuing rain, I could just make out the name of the place: "The Spinney". In a window to the right appeared a large "For Sale" sign.

"The place stands empty," the driver called down to me, "like I said. You'll be wanting an estate-agent to show you round."

I needed time on my own out here and, ignoring his suggestion, asked the man to return in an hour.

He signalled his understanding with a raise of his whip, cracked it above the horse, and drove off into the rain without another word.

The shower was beginning to thin. With my umbrella deflecting the spray, I tiptoed my way along the slippery flagstones to the shelter of the awning above the front porch. At a facing window, I thought I detected some sort of movement within; but I could not be certain. The house was supposed to be empty; and yet for some reason I proceeded to knock on the door as if someone might actually answer. Receiving no response, I waited a few moments and tried again.

Once it was clear that no one was coming, I tried turning the knob. Not unexpectedly, I found the door locked; and so once more hoisting my umbrella, I sloshed through the mud to the rear of the house.

A small overhang above the weathered back door offered some respite from the wet. Like the front door, this one too was locked; and yet it contained four window panes, the lower-left one of which had been broken.

The shattered window offered an opportunity. Employing little effort, one might insert an arm through the opening, reach down, and unlock the door from the inside. With the broken window as apparent evidence, I suspected that someone already had done just that—possibly, the woman I was seeking. A dark stone lying in the dirt a few feet away served to confirm my hypothesis.

"Hullo?" I cried through the opening. "Madame Costerd?"

All remained dark and silent within, leaving me little choice but to engineer the entrance I had imagined only seconds before. Carefully slipping my arm between the shards of remaining glass, I managed to grasp the lock, open the door, and slowly enter what I discovered to be a small lumber room. The window allowed just enough light for me to discern a bow-back chair, an empty ceramic planter, and a rolled-up rug.

Cautiously, I moved forward and, after passing through a gloomy, narrow corridor, found myself in the kitchen. A sash window brightened the room, and I could see a cooker and a small ice box. Though the room also contained a round, wooden table, it was neither the table nor even the dark-complexioned woman in the smoked glasses sitting at it that caught my eye. It was the pistol she was holding—an old Adams revolver—and, however shakily, it was pointed straight at me.

"Madame Costerd?" I ventured.

She nodded in reply. "Police?" she said in accented English.

"No. Someone who wants to help. I work with a private detective seeking answers. Perhaps you have heard the name, Sherlock Holmes."

"*Non*," she said coldly.

"In any case," I entreated, "could you please put down the gun?"

Her answer was to continue holding the pistol—and, I hasten to add, very inexpertly indeed. The barrel moved as she spoke. "How did you find me?"

I told her of the visit to her brother's house, the information gleaned from the nearby shops, and the discovery of her destination from the parcel dropped by the postman.

"Here in Kendal," she said, "I expected to find Emmeline, my friend—*mon amie*. I hoped for— *qu'est-ce que c'est? — l'asile,* asylum. I planned to remain hidden in her house; but as I have only just discovered, she passed last week. *Quel dommage.*"

I told Madame Costerd that the private detective and I were trying to find the murderer of the girl struck down at the British Museum.

"My daughter, you mean," she said listlessly. "Angelique was my daughter, *ma fille.*"

"Your daughter, you say? You'll pardon my frankness, Madame, but you look so different from the girl."

"Oh," the woman answered with quintessential French openness, "Angelique knew I had not given birth to her, but nonetheless she also knew that she was my daughter."

"Yet when you left your hotel," I countered, "you didn't bother to go to the museum. What mother allows her daughter to lie dead and alone on a cold floor?"

Madame Costerd bristled at my words. "I received a telegram to quit the hotel, to hide out. That's all I can tell you. I tried to leave as quickly as possible, but first I needed to find the photograph that Emerald had given me. I tore our rooms upside down to find it."

A photograph that "Emerald had given" her—here was the first connection between the French woman and Emerald Sommers.

"Whose photograph?" I asked, but the woman ignored me.

"Once I found it, I left." Pausing for the moment, she placed the Adams on the table, and I breathed a little easier. At the same time, she removed her smoked glasses, and a tear rolled out from beneath the drooping left eyelid. "I could not go to the Museum," she said defiantly. "I had to protect her."

"Protect that young girl? She was already dead."

"I knew Angelique had died. I mean, I had to protect Emerald."

"Mrs. Sommers? But what could have made you choose Mrs. Sommers over your daughter?"

Marie Costerd sat straight up and regarded the pistol. "I have said too much already. I cannot betray a confidence."

"Surely this has gone too far," I protested, taking a step forward.

The French woman picked up the pistol again and pointed it at me. "I assume it was the private detective you spoke of, this Sherlock Holmes, who put the notice about me in the newspaper. It made me leave the boarding house where I had taken a room. Now I expect you will notify the police that you have found me."

"First, I will notify my friend back in London."

She seemed to relax for the moment. "You must go. I tell you again, I cannot betray a confidence. I will say no more." With those words, she waved the Adams in the direction of the rear door. *"Vite."*

I understood the instruction and quickly retraced my steps out of the house. By then the rain had abated, and in a fine mist I walked slowly round the cottage, worrying all the while about the distraught woman I was leaving inside. I could not help wondering what Holmes would have done.

I slogged across the wet grounds towards the trees. A few minutes later, my cab reappeared; at the same time, the rain stopped.

"Decide to buy the place?" the driver shouted down to me with a wink.

Ignoring his attempt at humour, I told him to take me to the railway station. Not long thereafter, I was on my way back to London. Throughout the journey, I thought about little else than Madame Costerd and her secrets.

I had much to tell Sherlock Holmes, and yet when I returned to Baker Street there was still no sign of him. Following my adventure in Kendal, I quickly fell asleep.

Chapter Ten

Footsteps on the Stairs

The eye that pierces straightly to the future
Can never weep for joy.
             --Anna Katharine Green
             "Paul Isham"

"You were asleep when I came home last night," Sherlock Holmes greeted me Sunday morning. Sardines and toast graced the breakfast table in addition to the well-polished, silver-plated coffee-pot.

Minus hat and beard, Holmes was still outfitted in his workman's clothes; but though I wanted to hear what had kept him out so long, I felt my news more immediate. As he buttered his toast, I reported the details of my interview with Madame Costerd in Kendal the day before.

Holmes was particularly interested in the message the French woman had received just prior to exiting the hotel. "You say she actually mentioned the telegram that arrived after the girl was struck down, the one that prompted her to leave?"

Before I could answer, he put down his toast and sat upright in his chair. "Top hat and red beard—isn't that how Mrs. Rohlfs described the driver who had driven Emerald Sommers back to the Medallion?"

No sooner did I agree than Holmes rushed to one of the windows that overlooked Baker Street. Raising it, he leaned out and shouted, "Wiggins!" and within minutes I heard bounding up the stairs the footsteps of the leader of the Baker Street Irregulars, the band of street urchins who roamed the city under Holmes's employ.

"You there, slow down!" I heard Mrs. Hudson cry out vainly on the ground floor.

Wiggins entered the sitting room and bent over to catch his breath. With his baggy shirt and loose-fitting trousers, his tussled hair and dirty face, the lad appeared in the natural guise of the group, a uniform so ordinary as to go unnoticed.

"A hansom driver," Holmes instructed, "in the cab rank at the front of the British Museum." He furnished Wiggins with the brief but vivid description we had of the man, handed the boy some coins, and told him that, though it was Sunday and the museum was not open, he should ask about in order to bring the driver back to Baker Street. "The man's bound to be in the area."

Wiggins offered Holmes a stout military salute, and then he was gone.

Whilst the boy was carrying out his assignment, Holmes changed from his workman's clothes into his tweed jacket and trousers. Happily, he had rightly anticipated Wiggins' success, for within the hour, the tramp of heavy footfalls could be heard on the stairs.

"My name is Sherlock Holmes," my friend told the hansom driver for whom I had opened the door.

Top hat in hand, the man with the red beard smiled. "All of us at the museum know of you. Our neighbourhoods ain't that far apart. Your name is why I followed the lad. I am called Click."

"I have a question for you, Mr. Click," said Holmes. "I will, of course, pay you for your time."

Holmes went on to describe Mrs. Sommers and asked if he remembered her as a passenger who had taken his cab late Monday afternoon following the arrow-murder. "Take your time to consider."

"Don't need no time at all," Click said. 'I do remember her because I was expecting *two* fares when she come up with her friend; but in the end, it was only the one who climbed in."

"Do you recall her destination?" Holmes asked.

Click stroked his red beard. "Said she was going to the Medallion in High Holborn. I know the place. Fact is, I've taken many a fare to that hotel."

"Think carefully, man. Did you drive her directly there?"

"Funny you should ask, Mr. Holmes. It's what made the ride so strange—I mean, all anyone was talking about that evening was the terrible murder in the museum; and since the woman was coming from that very place and seemed unsteady on her feet, I reckoned she wanted to get home as quickly as possible. Yet between the museum and the Medallion she told me to stop in High Holborn."

Holmes looked at me with a quick smile. How he suspected that some curious activity had occurred was beyond my understanding. More astonishing was when he asked Click, "At 241?"

The driver raised his ginger eyebrows in amazement. "Just next door to 241—in front of the London Brew. She said she wanted to buy some coffee. Surprised me, I can tell you. I watched her go in, and I saw her come out a few minutes later with a parcel of coffee in hand. Then I drove her to the Medallion. She paid me and went inside."

"There's nothing sinister about buying a pound of coffee, Holmes," I observed. "Yet, as Mr. Click suggests, stopping to shop does indeed seem a bit strange after what the poor woman had gone through not long before."

"Number 241 is a telegraph office next door to London Brew," Holmes said. "Nothing could be simpler for Mrs. Sommers than to enter the coffeehouse, exit through the back, and walk into the telegraph office through its rear entrance."

To me, Holmes explained, "Mrs. Sommers could then send a telegram to her friend at Brown's urging her to leave. After which Mr. Click's passenger could return to the coffeehouse via the same route, purchase some coffee to verify her business, and then proceed in the cab to the hotel." Holmes turned to the driver. "Possible, Mr. Click?"

"Yes, indeed," he said, "though I don't have a clue what all this is about."

"Rest assured, Mr. Click," said Holmes offering him his pay, "there is no need for you to have any clue at all." My friend ushered the cab driver to the door. "Thank you very much indeed," Holmes said to the fellow.

"Now we know," Holmes said as soon as he and I were alone, "*how* Madame Costerd received her instructions to leave her hotel. *Why* is another matter."

We returned to our breakfasts to entertain that very question, but a new set of footsteps on the stairs cut short our plan. Opening the door, I greeted a dour Inspector Lestrade.

Holmes indicated that the policeman join us at table, and Lestrade removed his bowler and sat down. I offered him a plate, and he speared a few sardines and spread them upon a piece of toast.

"Thank you, Doctor," he said waving the food in my direction, "a welcome respite for a man forced to work on the Sabbath." He took a quick bite of his toast, then added, "But I cannot forget the point of my visit."

"Your prisoner Niven has confessed?" Holmes asked, his question laced with sarcasm.

"If only this case were that simple," Lestrade lamented. "Let me start with the positive news. One of my men tracked down the couple whose reported kissing had been stopped by the doorman. Amidst their blushes, they confirmed the story."

"One less suspect about whom to worry," I said.

Lestrade offered no smile, just an unenthusiastic nod. "I should also add that we found no evidence to justify holding Niven, so we released him as well."

"Reason hath prevailed," Holmes said.

"No need for mockery," Lestrade frowned as he finished his toast and wiped his hands clean upon a nearby napkin. "You will also be interested to know that the *Sûreté* have confirmed that Madame Costerd was indeed the mother of Angelique—although, in the name of fairness, they confessed they had been unable to locate a birth certificate which might prove the matter."

A missing birth certificate was consistent with Madame Costerd's admission to me that she herself had not given birth to the girl, a fact about which I had already informed Holmes.

"Most curious," said my friend. "But your furrowed brow suggests you have more worrisome news to share."

Lestrade pushed away his plate. "That's true, Mr. Holmes. I'm afraid I do have more to tell. Unfortunately, this British Museum case has taken an even uglier turn. The Met received a telegram this morning from the local constabulary in Kendal regarding the suspicious death of a woman."

"The suspicious death of a woman," Holmes repeated. "In Kendal, you say?" He spoke to Lestrade whilst looking at me.

I feared I knew what the inspector was about to announce and felt that I should inform him about my having been to Kendal the day before.

"Yesterday—" I began, yet Lestrade gave me little chance to speak.

"The Kendal Borough Police," he said quickly, "found a receipt dated 2nd June from

Brown's Hotel here in London. That's why they reckoned Scotland Yard would be interested."

I was about to try again, but the inspector held up a finger to silence me whilst he produced his notebook to confirm the major details. "They found the receipt in a house called 'The Spinney'."

He paused to pour himself a cup of coffee; as he did so, I realised I was dreading whatever he was about to say.

"It seems that the place in Kendal was visited late yesterday afternoon by an estate-agent and a prospective buyer. When they entered the premises, they discovered the body of a woman—quite dead, she was. Next to her lay—" here he perused his notes again— "an Adams six-shot revolver. All six chambers were empty, but there was only the one bullet that had been fired yesterday, the one that killed her."

Holmes had said that Marie Costerd had used five of those bullets to shoot out the face in the photograph. I now realised that she never had any intention of shooting me; she had saved the last bullet for herself.

"The woman was seated at the kitchen table," Lestrade continued. "As far as the police in Kendal could make out, she had leaned forward, held the gun to her right temple, and fired. Though her body slumped left, her arm prevented her from slipping to the floor. Instead she fell forward. The officers reported a lot of blood."

Part III

London

8 June 1890—11 June 1890

Chapter Eleven

Facts Revealed

For years an incident would germinate in my mind.
Then suddenly, perhaps in the night,
I would wake with my story conceived
from the first page to the last.
--Anna Katharine Green
Quoted by Kathleen Woodward
"Anna Katharine Green"
Bookman, October 1929

I cannot say that I was shocked to hear the news of Marie Costerd's suicide, not after seeing how distressed she had been in Kendal. I also reckoned it was well past time to let Lestrade know that I had met with the poor woman the day before, and so I finally informed him of the fact.

"Blimey!" he exclaimed, springing to his feet so frantically that he almost knocked over his chair. "You saw her *yesterday*?"

"I did."

"And you didn't tell me until now?"

"I tried, inspector; but before I was able, you broke the news about her suicide. She told me she had a secret to keep. I should imagine her death was the ultimate way of keeping it."

"Sit down, Lestrade," Holmes said. "Calm yourself. But a few days past, you told us that you already had your culprit—Niven Redmond. We believed you to be wrong and have been pursuing our own investigation."

Lestrade slowly took his seat, and we all settled into our coffees.

"Let me tell you what I have learned in the past twenty-four hours," Sherlock Holmes said. "I am convinced that it will bring this entire matter to a close."

Lestrade leaned back in his chair and sighed. I too was eager to hear.

"As you've already learned," Holmes said, "Director Aynesworth is having construction done to his home in Eaton Square. Specifically, he hired a team to tear down some interior walls. It seems he wants to replace armoires and wardrobes with built-in closets."

"Just like the rich Americans in New York I've read about," I said.

"Quite. In any case, after leaving you on Friday morning, Watson, I made some enquiries, found the house number, and marched right in and got to work. In the proper clothes and beard, I had no trouble blending in. Generally speaking, when a new bloke shows up and helps ease the load, workers are not too inquisitive."

"And just why did you do that, Mr. Holmes?" Lestrade asked. "What were you looking for inside the Director's house?"

"The coat Aynesworth wore the day of the murder."

"Again, the business with coats," Lestrade growled. "First, Niven; now, the Director."

"And the Curator," I added.

Lestrade glowered at the two of us. "What is it that you want? Why are those jackets—those coats—so bloody important?"

From a trouser pocket, Holmes withdrew the strip of black fabric Mrs. Rohlfs had given him and held it up for Lestrade to see. "We've been looking for the jacket-lining that contains any sign of a torn-away loop—this loop, actually." Holmes rolled the strip into a circle. "This piece of fabric was found in the room where the museum workers were sitting just before you questioned them."

"And no one saw fit to give it to me?" Lestrade complained.

Holmes handed the strip to Lestrade who unrolled it and turned it over to look at both sides. "If someone *had* given it to you," Holmes asked, "what would you have made of it?"

Lestrade shrugged.

"Allow me to offer a suggestion," said Holmes. "It's not too difficult to construe that, when sewn into a jacket to form a loop, such a strip might be used to secretly secure an arrow."

Lestrade re-examined the strip, turning it over again and then forming it into a circle as Holmes had done. With eyebrows raised, he looked up. "Like a tiny holster."

"Exactly," said Holmes, reclaiming the fabric and laying it on the table. "The frayed ends suggest that it was torn out, which presumably left corresponding marks on the inner lining."

Following along now, Lestrade nodded.

"I submit to you," Holmes continued, "that the killer used the loop, which he had crudely sewn into his jacket, to transport unseen a Norman arrow from the southern side of the museum where it was displayed to the other side where we already know the bow was hidden behind the tapestry. Niven's jacket didn't show any such tears; nor, as Watson discovered, did the Curator's. Thus, it was time to give the Director's coat a look-see—though first, of course, I had to find it.

"Now being a humble workman, I couldn't just open an armoire and look at the clothes within, especially not with the housekeeper hovering about. In fact, at no time on Friday did I get the opportunity to examine any of the Director's coats. I would need to try again the following day.

"Just as we labourers were set to leave, however, I saw Aynesworth arrive in the family carriage with a handsome young woman. With the weather having cleared, I noted earlier that a footman had set up a small table in the gardens behind the house, and it was to this spot I reckoned the couple would be going. Instead of leaving, I decided to circle back, position myself out of sight in a cavity exposed by the construction work, and hear what they had to say.

"I was correct in my surmise that Aynesworth and the lady would head for the garden. The two arrived and after Aynesworth dismissed the footman, they enjoyed their glasses of sherry. Then just like that, without further ado, Aynesworth told the young woman that he was terminating their engagement."

Lestrade and I both looked on in amazement.

"'It just won't work,' Aynesworth said, much to the young woman's dismay. He offered to pay her a settlement, but she stamped her foot and claimed to want only love. So put out was she that she immediately got up, re-entered the house, and apparently arranged for her own transportation home.

"Given my suspicions—as well as my ignorance—concerning the Director's plans, I positioned myself behind some trees in Eaton Square where I could maintain a vigil. I spent the entire night out there to be certain that I knew the man's whereabouts. In fact, I can reliably report that he never ventured out, and that is why I did not return home on Friday night.

"Fortunately, yesterday's early-morning rain did not amount to much. For breakfast I was able to get a meat-pudding from a nearby street vendor and return to the Director's house for work.

"Fortune continued to smile when the mid-morning sun broke through. Taking advantage of a crisp summer's afternoon, the housekeeper—no doubt in preparation for moving Aynesworth' garments into their new closets—decided to give them an airing. To that end, she took the wooden hangers holding Aynesworth's jackets, coats, and trousers and positioned them in neat order on a line in the clothes-yard behind the house.

"An opportunity presented itself when she went back inside. One end of the cord on which the clothing hung was tied to an exposed wood post, but the other end was attached to a small, metal hook on a rear wall of the house not far from where we workman passed. With the wind gusting as it was, I saw my chance. I exited the house, waited until no one was in sight and then loosened the knot.

"I proceeded to join some of the others cutting wood outside and waited for the wind to do its job. In a few minutes, a boisterous blast pulled at the hanging clothes. Billowing like full sails, they caused the knot to come undone. In a moment, all the grey jackets and coats and trousers so precisely hung by the housekeeper pitched to the ground in a jumble of cloth.

"I was upon them in an instant. Though no one else had made a move towards the pile of clothes, I told my fellow labourers, 'It's all right, I'll pick 'em up."

I knew I had to hurry because the moment the housekeeper noticed what had happened, she would come rushing out. Happily, it took just three grey coats before I found what I was looking for.

"Shielded from view, I pulled off my baggy coat and donned the article I had found, covered it with my own, re-affixed the cord, and replaced the fallen clothes." Pausing to take a breath, Holmes pointed across the room. "That's Aynesworth's coat on the desk, the one I appropriated."

A clever sleight of hand on Holmes's part, I thought, but Lestrade cried out, "Are you mad? You stole Director Aynesworth's coat?" The inspector rose to his feet. "I can't be party to such nonsense, Mr. Holmes, especially not with a swell like Leonard Aynesworth. You private investigators may be able to bend the law, and from time to time I may even ignore your illegalities; but I cannot allow myself to be a party to them." With that, he turned away from his chair and marched out, slamming the door behind him.

Holmes pulled a face. "Poor Lestrade. Yet again he has wasted the opportunity to solve the case."

A knock on our door seemed to punctuate Holmes's assessment. In actuality, it announced the arrival of Billy the page.

"A note for you, Dr. Watson," he surprised me by saying as he handed me a folded piece of paper. I waited till the lad had exited and then opened the message. It was from the nurse attending Mrs. Sommers. Her patient had come round. "'She's able to speak,'" I read aloud. "'The doctor will be out tomorrow.'"

Holmes clapped his hands together. "At last," he said. "The very person who should be able to tell us what the Director had in mind. I do believe that the death of her friend Marie Costerd should be impetus enough."

"But what about Aynesworth's coat?" I asked.

"Ah, yes, Aynesworth's coat—the key to the solution." Holmes strode to the desk and picked up the article in question. Clearing away the dishes, he laid the coat on the table and spread the lapels wide to expose its silver lining.

"Do you see them, Watson?" he asked, directing my attention to a narrow set of tiny holes and small tears about an inch apart above the inside breast-pocket displaying Aynesworth's monogram.

Retrieving the cloth strip from where he had left it on the table, Holmes held it in a circular fashion, placing its tiny holes and wisps of thread atop the corresponding holes and strands in the lining. "You see?"

"A match," I replied, "though I suppose an expert barrister might argue such evidence is circumstantial."

Holmes folded the coat. "We may worry about courtrooms later. On the morrow we will hear from Mrs. Sommers. I am certain her testimony is essential to resolving the entire problem."

"Why not bring along Mrs Rohlfs?" I suggested. "She befriended Mrs. Sommers at the Hastings exhibition. Perhaps her presence will comfort the woman and make speaking easier."

"The very thing, Watson. Let us discuss our plans further during dinner at Simpson's."

Chapter Twelve

Mrs. Sommers' Story

I met thee, dear, and love thee—yet we part,
Thou on thine unknown way and I on mine,
Ere the music of my woman's heart
Has had full time to harmonize with thine.
                    Anna Katharine Green
                    "In Farewell"
                    The Defence of the Bride

Monday afternoon the nurse called Nelly took the two Rohlfs children to a band concert in Regent's Park. Earlier in the day Charles Rohlfs had left Brown's for shops in Tottenham Court Road as part of his self-styled survey of British furniture.

"He has appointments at Oetzmann's and Shoolbred and Company," Mrs. Rohlfs told us. "Later, he's going to Harry Lebus in the East End. Charles is particularly interested in the Arts and Crafts movement, and he says that Lebus has much in that line." Smoothing the folds of her purple frock, she announced, "All this is to say, gentlemen, that I am free for the interview with Emerald Sommers."

"Splendid," Holmes replied, rubbing his hands together in anticipation.

At Brown's, the doorman in plush livery secured a growler, which transported us to the Medallion Family Hotel in High Holborn. Seated as we were in the carriage, we made quite the group—

a consulting detective, a writer of detective fiction, and a medical doctor—a triumvirate ready, or so one hoped, for all manner of exigencies.

It was the nurse who opened the door to the drawing room. Mrs. Sommers, ensconced on a blue velveteen settee, sat cloaked in a burgundy-coloured wrapper. With strands askew, her black hair looked hastily put together; yet as she sat motionlessly with her hands clasped in her lap, she appeared quite dignified and composed.

She greeted Mrs. Rohlfs with a brief smile of recognition, and after Mrs. Rohlfs introduced Holmes and me, Mrs. Sommers indicated we all be seated.

As the nurse had informed us, there was no sign of the doctor; and once the nurse had exited to the bedroom, Mrs. Sommers appeared ready to talk.

As Holmes and I had awaited the silver trolley at Simpson's the previous night, he had asked me to serve as the messenger of sad tidings at today's meeting. Thus, I began, "We're sorry to have to open this conversation with more tragic news, Mrs. Sommers, but your friend, Marie Costerd, is dead."

The woman stared off at nothing in particular, her jaw set, her eyes steely. There were no tears or other outward displays of emotion. Perhaps, they had been used up.

"We extend our condolences to you, Madam," I offered.

Sherlock Holmes spoke more directly. "Marie Costerd killed herself, Mrs. Sommers."

At dinner the night before, he had told me that he intended his bluntness to provoke a reaction.

"She shot herself in the head with an Adams revolver," he continued, "rather than confess an apparent secret involving the two of you. She shot herself in the home of Emmeline Ford with the same pistol she had used to decimate a photograph containing the facial features of an unknown man."

Mrs. Sommers's eyes flickered at the news. "Marie was a true friend to the last," she said softly. "She deserved a better end than the one I created for her. Her death makes it all the more necessary that I explain our sad history."

"When did you first meet Marie?" Mrs. Rohlfs asked. "If you don't mind telling us," she added gently.

"Marie and I attended a convent school near Canterbury when we were young. Her French parents wanted her as far away from them as possible. It's where she learned her English. In my case, my mother had died in childbirth; and my father had little interest in raising a daughter. Most of the girls had similar tales to tell. Emmeline was another friend, but Marie and I were the ones who used to play together whenever we had the chance.

"As we grew older, our thoughts turned to more adult conventions. It was not long before Marie and I discovered that we had both become infatuated with the same man, our young French instructor called Eugène. With Marie's French background, she had much more in common with him than I, but I was more attractive in those years. After all, the poor creature had that drooping eyelid and olive complexion." Mrs. Sommers smiled. "I knew I could manipulate the naive fellow—not a noble

153

confession, I admit, but the truth, nonetheless. Indeed, so successful was I in pursuing the man that once Marie and I both became of age, I expected Eugène to ask me to marry him."

"How did Marie take this development?" Mrs. Rohlfs asked. "Certainly, she must have been aware of what was going on."

"Girls talk, as I am certain you well know. We were rivals for the same man, to be sure; but I am proud to say that our friendship was stronger. As devoted to him as I recognised Marie was, I could not allow myself to break her heart. And so I ended my relationship with the French instructor; and as I sensed he would, he turned his attention to Marie and eventually married her."

"His full name?" Holmes asked.

"Eugène Costerd."

"Of course," Holmes murmured. "Emil's brother."

"Eugène and Marie moved to Paris. He secured a job in a school; but within their first year together, before they could start a family, he died of some sort of heart ailment."

"A tragic tale," I acknowledged, "but how did Marie's story continue to affect your own?"

Mrs. Sommers took a deep breath. "After my own schooling ended, I worked in a bakery in Canterbury. It was there that I met a most charming fellow. He had come from London with his mother to tour the cathedral and stopped in the bakery for biscuits for the two of them. Even then, at the start, I thought mother and son seemed a trifle too close— if you take my meaning. In any case, I knew I was not of his class, not with his fine clothes and obvious education.

"And yet his winsome nature lingered in my mind, and the next weekend he returned and, to my great joy, asked me to dinner. We discovered we had lots in common—a love of Shakespeare, for instance.

"'Your favourite play?' I asked him.

"'You first,' he said.

"'*Romeo and Juliet.*'

"'Mine too,' he grinned."

"Of course," Holmes murmured again.

"Before we knew it, we were spending lots of time together—too much time together."

"This fellow," I said, "his surname was Sommers?"

"No, Doctor," she smiled, "Sommers is my own family name." Silence followed her pronouncement.

Mrs. Rohlfs attempted another line of enquiry. "What did his mother have to say about your meetings?" It was obvious the crime writer knew how to secure the essentials of an engrossing story.

Mrs. Sommers raised her clasped hands and smiled. "Oh, that was clear enough. She wanted her son to have nothing to do with me. Through her own social circles, she went so far as to set up a match for him, a stylish young woman from a well-to-do family. But he wouldn't listen to such a plan. His mother, he told me, wasn't going to decide his life. No, he saw us as a modern couple—so much so, that in a small vicarage a few miles outside of Canterbury, we married.

"How much did he love me? As testimony to his commitment, he insisted that we have a reference to *Romeo and Juliet* engraved inside my wedding ring. We chose my favourite passage—Juliet's that begins, 'My bounty is as endless as the sea . . . .' The three lines are too long to fit within a ring, of course, so we settled on the numerical reference instead."*

(The nurse had obviously committed a capital blunder when she related Mrs Sommers' ravings to the mutinous ship, *Bounty*; the woman's comments were instead a quotation from Shakespeare.)

"And his mother's reaction to your marriage?" Mrs. Rohlfs persisted.

"He didn't tell her."

"Not at first, you mean," said Mrs. Rohlfs.

Mrs. Sommers looked down at her bare ring finger. "Not ever." She spoke the words quietly. "At first, he said he hoped to keep our marriage secret for just a short while. It bothered me, of course, especially following our weekends together in Canterbury when he would return to London for the days in between. As I had initially suspected, he wasn't very strong; and eventually the web his mother spun became too great for him to evade. He agreed to marry her choice and to make our own match disappear."

"But that would make him a bigamist," I exclaimed. "Surely—"

---

* II, ii, 133-135.
"My bounty is as boundless as the sea,
My love as deep; the more I give to thee,
The more I have, for both are infinite."

"One morning," she continued, "I woke to discover that my husband, as well as my wedding ring, had disappeared. Later that same day, I learned of a fire in the vicarage that destroyed the parish records."

"Still, the vicar would know," I countered.

Mrs. Sommers sighed. "He'd gone off somewhere—I didn't know to where. And it would still be only his word. There's no actual proof. Besides, money has a way of silencing people."

"And thus," I observed, "your husband disowned your marriage vows; all history of your union was cancelled."

"Not entirely *all*, Doctor," Mrs. Sommers replied, her features taking on a strange mix of sadness and defiance. "You see, by that time, I discovered I was with child."

"Oh, my poor dear," said Mrs. Rohlfs, leaning forward to lay a hand on the woman's arm.

"I knew that I was too distraught to become a mother, especially with the father gone. Desperate for advice, I travelled to Paris to explain my condition to the one person who would understand, my dearest friend Marie. And right then, we decided that when the baby was born, Marie, though agreeing that at some point I might still claim the child, would raise the baby in Paris as her own. Within a few months, I had a little girl, and Marie named her—"

"Angelique," Mrs. Rohlfs whispered.

"My word," I said as connections among the various participants in the sad story began to solidify.

"Oh, you were quite correct earlier, Dr. Watson," Mrs. Sommers agreed, "by marrying the woman his mother had selected for him, my husband did indeed commit bigamy. But I had no proof; and seeing little point in disrupting his new marriage with scandal, I remained silent. For sixteen years I remained silent. I procured an education for myself and worked as a governess for a kind family whilst Marie raised Angelique as her own.

"But then I read in *The Times* that my husband's wife had died and that he sought to marry once more—some young woman who didn't suspect a thing. That's when I said, 'Enough,' and finally decided to confront the man. Hoping to render his life as empty as my own, I wrote to him demanding that he marry no one else or risk my coming forward. I knew he was of high social standing and that attaching scandal to his name could bring him down."

"The child?" asked Mrs. Rohlfs. "Did you tell him that he was the girl's father?"

"No," she said, "but I planned to. Actually, I wanted to surprise him with his beautiful girl before this second, ill-planned marriage could take place. Who knows? Perhaps I even held onto the foolish vision that we might all live together as a family."

"And such thinking led you to the British Museum last week," Holmes observed.

"Yes. To his credit—or his fear—he agreed he would break off his new engagement, and he wrote to me here at the Medallion in late May. We could talk things over where he worked, he said—at the Battle of Hastings Exhibition in the North Hall of the British Museum one week from that day. At precisely one o'clock on the second of June, he would meet me at the quiver of arrows by the balustrade overlooking the central stairs.

"How silly was I. I had come to believe that our meeting would present the perfect opportunity to introduce him to his beautiful daughter. I wrote as much to Marie and asked her to bring Angelique to London. God forgive me, I told Marie to have Angelique come on her own to the appointed spot in the North Hall. Curse the day I did so. All worked according to plan until—well, you know what happened. The poor girl leaped in front of me and was struck by that horrible arrow, the arrow of death."

"The arrow," Holmes said, "that was clearly intended for you."

Chapter Thirteen

A Confession

*. . . After the period of formulating a plot is passed,
I regard the whole operation with surprise,
and wonder how it all came to me.*
--Anna Katharine Green
Quoted by T. Fisher Unwin,
*Good Reading About
Many Books
Mostly by their Authors*

*N*one of us disagreed with Holmes. It was the only logical conclusion. Mrs. Rohlfs did what she could to comfort Mrs. Sommers; and after calling in the nurse to care for her patient, I indicated we three questioners should now leave the poor woman in peace.

"Did you notice how Mrs. Sommers never mentioned the man's name?" asked Mrs. Rohlfs as we exited the Medallion.

"Protecting him even now," I said as Holmes hailed a cab.

I assumed we would be depositing Mrs. Rohlfs at her hotel. Sherlock Holmes, however, had an alternative plan.

"Islington!" he shouted to the driver once we had all climbed into the carriage. "The Van Dyck Photography Studio in Upper Street."

After a drive of some twenty minutes, the cab rolled to a stop in front of the small shop belonging to photographer Edward Russell. Moments after hurrying inside, Holmes returned to the carriage with a small yellow envelope. "Brown's Hotel," he told the driver before climbing in.

As the carriage lurched forward, he said, "We don't need Mrs. Sommers to speak the name of her husband, not when we have this." He held up the envelope to underscore his point.

The seal-flap had been tucked inside the cover rather than pasted shut. Holmes laid the envelope in his lap and after carefully sliding out the flap, withdrew the photograph. The picture remained hidden beneath a small sheet of thin white paper.

It took only an instant before we all found ourselves staring at a sepia-coloured image of a man with sharp features, narrow eyes, and silver hair, his head tilted at the same angle we recognised in the fringes of the photograph obliterated by Marie Costerd.

"Leonard Aynesworth," Holmes said, breaking the hush. "I believe that this photograph, along with the coat I was able to acquire, will convince Lestrade to act. Tomorrow morning should be soon enough."

Minutes later, Holmes escorted Mrs. Rohlfs into Brown's. He spent a few moments conversing with her in the lobby before returning to our carriage.

It had been a dramatic day, and by the time we arrived in Baker Street I was ready for sleep. No sooner did we walk into the sitting room, however, than Sherlock Holmes eyed his violin case. "I think Paganini is in order," he said as he opened the case and picked up the instrument. "Are you aware of the rumours that surround the man?"

Knowing full well how much Holmes loved to tell anecdotes about the infamous musician, I none the less asked, "What rumours?"

Holmes waved the bow in my direction. "'The Devil's violinist' people called him."

"What rumours?" I repeated.

Holmes raised his bushy eyebrows. "The strings of Paganini's violin were said to have been fashioned from the bowstrings of a Barbarian tribe in northern Italy. If you trust such tales, old fellow, you'll believe that before the strings reached Paganini's violin, they helped kill hundreds of people."

Attempting to fall asleep to the lilting strains of Paganini's *Caprice No. 24*, I realised I had been wrong. However melodic the tune, there would be no respite this night from the flight of fateful arrows.

Q

Tuesday, 10 June. The police van entered Eaton Square one week and a day following the murder of Angelique Costerd.

"That's the one," Holmes said, his long forefinger pointing out to Lestrade and me the white, four-storey house where two days earlier he had worked on the renovation of closets.

With Holmes's promise to lay out the case against Leonard Aynesworth, Lestrade had calmed down from the outrage he had felt the day before. In fact, he admitted that the Yard had done some productive investigating of their own. "If I am convinced by your arguments today," he told us, "I assure you that I am prepared to make an arrest."

The carriage rolled to a stop, and the three of us stepped out, Holmes carrying a brown-paper package under his right arm; Lestrade, a Gladstone bag. We followed the inspector to the japanned outer door where a pull of the bell brought the butler.

"Police," said Lestrade, "here for Mr. Aynesworth."

"I'll see if he's in," sniffed the butler, set to close the door.

In the finest tradition of coppering, however, Lestrade raised his foot over the threshold and stationed it just within the entry hall. The door could not be closed. "We'll wait inside," he announced, "thank you very much."

"All of us," Holmes added.

Moments later Aynesworth appeared, his eyebrows raised in surprise at seeing us gathered as we were. "What brings you here, gentlemen? More news about the tragic incident at the Museum?"

"Quite right, sir," replied Lestrade. "We have a few additional matters we'd like to straighten out."

Aynesworth raised an arm in the direction of the library and ushered us into a wood-panelled room replete with richly filled bookshelves that climbed to the ceiling. A red-leather couch and a pair of matching wing chairs faced a highly-polished desk.

Against a side wall stood a small, round table whose white-marble top held a number of photographs. Though I recognised few faces, I did see a photograph of Aynesworth with the Prime Minister and another with the Lord Mayor of London. On the wall above the pictorial display hung a black-framed mirror.

"How may I help you?" the Director asked. His words sounded amiable, yet he made no indication that we should sit down.

"May I?" asked Holmes, gesturing to place the brown-paper package on the desk.

"Be my guest," Aynesworth said, watching Holmes's movements all the while.

"Now then, Mr. Aynesworth," began Lestrade, "we've done some checking on the backgrounds of the individuals connected to this case. Of all the persons located in the North Hall on the day of the murder, you appear to have been the closest to the staircase by the Curator's office—that is, the stairs we suspect the killer used to escape his upper-floor hideaway."

"Surely there were others in the vicinity," Aynesworth countered. "I saw them. That couple in the corner, for instance—and the doorman who questioned them."

"Oh, yes," Lestrade grinned, "there were others. Perhaps I misspoke. What I should have said was, you were the only one in the vicinity burdened with incriminating evidence."

Aynesworth responded with what could only be described as a smirk.

"For example," Lestrade continued, "as soon as I learned that you were once a member of the mountaineering group, the Alpine Club, I sent a man over to their headquarters in St. Martin's Place.*

"The Club just off Trafalgar Square?" he asked, running a hand through his silver hair. "Indeed, I was a member—still am, in fact. No crime in that, I should imagine. I like the odd climb now and again. I trekked about more in my younger years than I do now, of course."

"It was actually those younger years that intrigued us most at Scotland Yard—in particular, your participation in adjunct sporting contests. According to the records of the club, you were quite the expert with bow and arrow. Won a few archery tournaments, in fact. There was a competition in Nottingham, for example."

"Ah, yes," Aynesworth recalled with a smile. Now that you mention it, I do recall winning that contest though I haven't participated in the sport for many years."

Lestrade nodded and turned to my friend. "Mr. Holmes, perhaps you would like to pick up the narrative at this point."

Sherlock Holmes stepped forward. "I suggest, Mr. Aynesworth," he said in his most

---

* It would be another five years before the Alpine Club moved to 23 Savile Row next to the arched passageway to Conduit Street.

imperious tone, "that just recently you found a cast-off Norman bow in your Curator's storage cellar."

Aynesworth shrugged. "I have cause to examine many artifacts that we have placed there. I may have picked up such a bow, but I don't—"

"I further suggest that not only did you examine the bow, but that you carried it up from the cellar and set it in the back of the Curator's closet where it couldn't be seen."

Aynesworth furrowed his brow. "If it couldn't be seen, then how—?"

"The charwoman reported that she had discovered it there by accident."

"The charwoman," Aynesworth repeated contemptuously.

"I further suggest that sometime before the second of June, you carried that bow up the Curator's private stairway to the upper-floor gallery of the North Hall—in particular, the gallery that houses the wall-hanging—and that you placed the bow in the doorway behind the tapestry until the time came for you to use it."

Chin thrust upward, Aynesworth maintained an arrogant pose.

"Perhaps, you should take a look at this," Holmes said, placing his fingers in his waistcoat pocket.

A wave of troubled curiosity crossed Aynesworth's face.

With a dramatic flair that one might trace back to his days on the stage, Holmes produced the strip of black fabric, which he raised above his head for all present to observe.

At the sight of the black strip, Aynesworth's demeanour changed. His face seemed to sag and his shoulders droop.

"You should be interested to know, Mr. Aynesworth," said Holmes, still holding high the little strip of cloth, "that thanks to a bit of swan's feather, we believe that this piece of cloth was sewn into the lining of a coat —rather clumsily, I might add—to form a small loop. Out of sight in that loop was hung an arrow, so that it could be carried in the coat unseen from the southern side of the museum to the northern in order to partner with the hidden bow on their deadly mission."

"Sheer humbug," Aynesworth managed to sputter. "That fragment of cloth proves nothing. Yours is a ridiculous hypothesis, Mr. Holmes, a hairbrained theory concocted to accuse a hapless victim of a terrible crime, a crime for which you obviously have no real suspects."

As Aynesworth spoke, Holmes made his way to the desk, raised the parcel he had left there, and began to unwrap it. Slowly emerging from beneath the layers of brown paper was the coat that Holmes had taken from the Director's house. Unfolding the garment, Holmes opened wide its lapels and displayed for Aynesworth the monogram bearing the Director's initials on the inner breast-pocket.

"Your coat I'm certain you will agree."

"Yes, but—"

Holmes indicagted the needle marks just above the pocket where the loop had once been attached to the grey lining. To emphasise his point, he produced a safety pin with which he affixed the strip to its original spot. Doffing his own jacket, he nodded at Lestrade. The inspector withdrew from his Gladstone one of the Norman arrows featured in the Hastings exhibit and handed it to Holmes.

"You stole that jacket," Aynesworth charged, in an obvious attempt to undermine the demonstration.

Lestrade's face flushed, but an undeterred Sherlock Holmes inserted the arrow into the loop, hooked the bodkin arrowhead to the top of the strip, and slipped his arms into the sleeves. Even though the skirt of the coat was short for a man above six feet in height, Holmes gracefully stretched out his arms, turned about, and displayed how easily an arrow conveyed in such a manner could be hidden.

"Thus was the murderous dart brought to the gallery in which the bow was concealed," Holmes announced, "the same gallery in which an accomplished archer—you, Mr. Aynesworth—crouched behind the left-hand pedestal, strung the bow, and shot the arrow that ended the life of a young girl.

"You made your escape down the Curator's staircase in your regular street-shoes, hoping that no one would be in the Curator's office in the middle of the afternoon. It was a risk, to be sure, but a chance you deemed worth taking. The Curator's stairs provided concealment compared to the small staircase at the rear of the exhibit—where, had you reached it, you would have encountered the attendant, Niven Redmon. In point of fact, you almost made it to the exit—exactly where you told Inspector Lestrade you were when the arrow was sent. It was the girl's scream and the order to lock the doors that did you in."

The Hastings Director shook his head and, turning to the table behind him, reached for one of the small, framed pictures. Only then did I see that it contained a half-tone newspaper portrait of the murdered girl.

"Why would I want to kill this child?" questioned Aynesworth as he held up the portrait. "Look here. I am so distressed by her death that I keep this picture to remind me of the heinous deed that happened under my responsibility. I could never kill anyone, let alone an innocent child. What can you be thinking?"

"Actually, Mr. Aynesworth," answered Holmes, "I don't believe that killing the young girl was your intention. I think you had another target in mind, and tragically the girl had got in the way."

"And just who might that other target have been, Mr. Holmes?" Aynesworth demanded as he returned the photograph to its place beneath the mirror.

"Me," came the answer.

All heads turned towards the doorway.

"*I* was your target, Leonard."

Shockingly, the response had been delivered by Emerald Sommers who now stood a few feet in front of Mrs. Rohlfs. Now I understood what Holmes and the American woman had discussed in the lobby at Brown's the previous evening whilst I waited in the growler.

Holmes had arranged for her to bring Mrs. Sommers to Eaton Square in a second carriage just after we arrived with Lestrade. The two ladies had trailed behind us on the road, entered the house after we did, and remained out of sight in the corridor leading to the library. I now also understood what Holmes had meant when he told the butler to allow entry for "all of us".

Aynesworth walked quickly to Mrs. Sommers and extended his hands. "Emerald," he whispered.

She stood motionless, her face drawn. "I want to hear it from your lips, Leonard. I want to hear you say you shot that arrow."

"I never—oh, let me tell you what I intended to say when I arranged our meeting at the museum. I had a most serious question to ask you then—and now."

Mrs. Sommers' eyes smouldered. "Tell me you shot the arrow, Leonard."

Though like Mrs. Sommers, I too wanted to hear the man confess, I readily admit that I also wanted to hear what he was now claiming he had hoped to offer her that terrible afternoon.

Once more, the Director smoothed his silver hair. The man who had just broken off his third engagement took both hands of the woman standing before him and brought them up to his heart. He took a breath and said, "Will you marry me, Emerald?"

Too noble to be distracted by so astounding an offer, Mrs. Sommers shook her hands free. "You don't understand what you've done, do you, Leonard? Even now. You must know that I recognised you as soon as I saw you in the museum when I was holding the poor girl in my arms. Still,

I couldn't denounce you—my husband—not even when the police thought I myself had stabbed her—not even when I realised that the arrow you let loose was intended for me."

Mrs. Sommers grasped Aynesworth's lapels and pulled him towards her. "Listen to me, Leonard." Their faces were inches apart. "Know that the girl, Angelique, that beautiful child whom you murdered—know this, Leonard Aynesworth—that girl was your daughter. Marie Costerd may have raised her, but she was your child."

She let go of the man, and he staggered back as if he had been struck.

"God knows I did my best, Leonard. I even left Marie your picture should the need have arisen to show Angelique her father. That scream you heard in the museum, the scream that prompted the call for the doors to be locked—it did not come from the poor girl. The arrow you shot made certain she was beyond uttering a sound; that cry came from me, her mother, once I realised what you had done."

At last, the timing made sense. The mother's shriek came minutes *after* the arrow had struck, not simultaneously as it would have if the poor victim had been able to scream out. Those vital extra moments allowed the Director to run down the stairs to the Curator's office and onto the ground floor. Fortunately, young Niven Redmond had recognised the anguish in the *cri de coeur* and called for the exhibition hall to be shut down. A few seconds later and Aynesworth would have been out the door.

For his part, the Director stood speechless. He looked back at the girl's picture on the table and then into the mirror.   Along with Leonard Aynesworth, we all now saw in the reflection the same narrow eyes, the same straight nose, and the same high cheekbones that appeared in the newspaper portrait.

No one moved until the man dropped down into a chair. "I—I—I didn't know," he stammered.

"And if you had," Mrs. Sommers demanded, "would it have made a difference?"

Before Aynesworth could answer, Inspector Lestrade placed a solid hand on the man's shoulder.

Rather than laying blame, I speak in the abstract.   A writer of romance fiction might have recognised in the previous scene the opportunity to highlight the love story and lessen the violence. To lessen the brutality, such a writer might allow the villain to escape society's most drastic punishment by presenting him with more compassionate alternatives—say, poison in a hidden vial or a private moment with a pistol or even, dare I suggest, death outright from shock.

Such a writer might also make much of the little mahogany box with the heart-design carved into the lid that Holmes found on the mantel. Opening the box revealed the wedding ring Aynesworth had hidden away after having taken it from his wife's finger all those years ago in Canterbury, the golden band that contained the engraved reference to *Romeo and Juliet.* Such a writer might even have had Emerald put the ring back on her finger.

Yet I would argue that in tempering the death sentence, such writers protect their readers from the cruel and violent lessons reality has to offer. In our real world, no soft ending presented itself to the killer of Angelique Costerd.

Mr. Leonard Aynesworth—scion of a rich family, director of museum exhibitions, possible candidate for Parliament, and a heartless, scheming bigamist—was found guilty of murder in the Old Bailey and hanged at Her Majesty's Prison, Wandsworth, in March of 1892.

Chapter Fourteen

Resolution

I am just simple enough in my hero-worship to feel satisfied
that I have been able to distinguish myself sufficiently
to have received heart letters from such masters
as [William] Gladstone and Wilkie Collins.
-- Anna Katharine Green
Quoted by Agnes Repellier
"A Tribute"
Life, October 11, 1906

"*I*'m grateful to you fellows for involving Kitty in your investigation," said Charles Rohlfs to Holmes and me the following day. Beneath his flat cap, a broad smile illuminated his round face. Mrs. Rohlfs was off playing with the children, allowing us a moment alone with her husband. "The purpose of this trip," he confided, "was to cheer Kitty up following the loss of her father. She might appear strong, but emotions sometimes get the better of her. That she helped solve a murder and strengthen the pillars of justice in the process makes it all the better."

"I assure you, Mr. Rohlfs," replied Holmes, "the terrible crime we had to confront was in no way intended—as you so cavalierly put it— 'to cheer her up'."

Charles Rohlfs looked wounded. "I certainly did not intend to sound callous, Mr. Holmes."

My friend brushed away the comment. "Let me tell you this, Mr. Rohlfs," said Sherlock Holmes, "your wife—or should I say, Anna Katharine Green—is quite the detective."

"Coming from you of all people, sir," he beamed, "that is quite the compliment."

The day after the murder of Angelique Costerd had been resolved, Mrs. Rohlfs invited Holmes and me to join the family for a picnic at the outdoor tables near the Zoological Gardens in Regent's Park. Though Holmes would not partake in such frivolity, he did agree to a post-prandial walk following our own lunch in Baker Street and allowed that such a perambulation might well terminate in the nearby park. If we should happen to encounter the Rohlfs family during our outing through the greens, well, so be it.

Encounter the family we did, of course. When we first arrived, Mrs. Rohlfs and her husband were sitting on a wooden bench next to a now-closed food hamper watching the children dart about. After Mrs. Rohlfs hailed us, she rose, introduced her husband, and then summoned the children so we could meet them as well.

With his wife still off cavorting with Rosamund and Sterling, Charles told us about his own activities in London. From a nearby rucksack, he withdrew a foot-tall model of a wooden chair which he was in the process of carving. The model reflected what would eventually become his signature dramatic style of chair-design: a low base, a small seat, and a very narrow, high back containing ascending and plummeting swirls and seraphs.

"I helped him with those curves and spirals," Mrs. Rohlfs said upon re-joining us. "One day Charles will put the full-scale versions on the market."

Quite an artistic couple, I thought, each helping the other, he a former actor, she an accomplished writer, two empathetic souls raising a family together. It was just such sensitivity, I judged, that led to the debilitating illness that rendered Mrs. Rohlfs bedridden during the final week of June. Such can be the cost to the compassionate heart of rooting about in a murder investigation, especially one involving the death of an innocent young soul.[*]

As for the other major players in the drama, we never again saw young Stanford, the love-struck suitor who had fallen for the beautiful French girl though we did hear something from Lestrade about Mrs. Sommers' continuing to mourn her lost daughter whilst attempting to find suitable homes for forlorn orphans. I am certain that her late friend Marie Costerd would have approved.

A final word: However much Mrs. Rohlfs had grieved for the dead in our recent case—not to

---

[*] Green's illness in London during late June of 1890 is also reported by Joseph Cunningham in *The Artistic Furniture of Charles Rohlfs.*

mention her sympathy for Mrs. Sommers, the poor survivor—I feared from the start that the intertwined tragedies of these women might simply be too appealing for a successful writer like Anna Katharine Green to ignore, that our true-life investigation into the horrible murder at the British Museum could not fail to provide inspiration for a crime writer in search of a saleable plot.

To be sure, Anna Katharine Green undertook countless liberties in her novel to maintain the anonymity of actual events. She changed names. She created false characters. She provided her villain a simplistic demise. She introduced melodramatic storms amidst mountain chasms and shadowy silhouettes darting among the lightning strikes. She even went so far as to substitute a Wild West exhibition in a New York gallery for the Battle of Hastings presentation in the Northern Hall of the British Museum. Apache arrows replaced those of the Normans.

And yet in fairness to the American lady, I must also add that in spite of all those literary fantasies, in the end she could not prevent herself from revealing a singular but telling link to historical reality.

In Mrs. Rohlfs's fictional version of the investigation, Caleb Sweetwater, Inspector Gryce's aforementioned assistant, learns from the museum-director's chauffeur (who plays much the same role in Mrs. Rohlfs's novel that my eavesdropping friend did in actuality) of the Director's plan to break off his latest marital engagement. Anna Katharine Green, unable to ignore all the facts in so significant a development—or, perhaps, as a kind of unheralded tribute to the truth—bestowed upon the sleuthing chauffeur the revelatory appellation of "Holmes".

THE END

Editor's Notes

To appreciate more fully Watson's account of the so-called "British Museum murder," one should read Anna Katharine Green's version of events in *The Mystery of the Hasty Arrow*. Originally published by Dodd, Mead, and Company in 1917, the book is also available in recent reprints.

For a biography of Anna Katharine Green and literary analyses of her books, see *Mother of Detective Fiction: The Life and Works of Anna Katharine Green* by Patricia D. Maida.

For detailed information on the relationship between Charles Rohlfs and Anna Katharine Green, see Joseph Cunningham's *The Artistic Furniture of Charles Rohlfs*. As the title implies, the focus of the book is on the creativity of Charles, and yet Cunningham does note that in the month after recovering from the illness in June 1890 documented by Watson, Anna and her family toured Canterbury. In spite of Cunningham's detailed descriptions of the couple's activities in England, he makes no mention of whether Charles's wife spent any of her time in Canterbury researching the story of Emerald Sommers' early life there or locating the convent-school attended by the three close friends, Emerald, Marie, and Emmeline.

A number of studies discuss the importance of Anna Katharine Green not only in the history of the murder mystery, but also as a frequently-overlooked female writer of the late-nineteenth century. These include Catherine Ross Nickerson's *The Web of Iniquity: Early Detective Fiction by American Women* (see "Anna Katharine Green and the Gilded Age") and Lucy Sussex's *Women Writers and Detectives in Nineteenth-Century Crime Fiction* (see "The Art of Murder: Anna Katharine Green").

The papers of Anna Katharine Green can be found in the Humanities Research Center of the University of Texas at Austin.